# MARRIED TO A DISTINGUISHED THUG

## SHVONNE LATRICE

# About the Author

### <u>Other Works by Me:</u>

Good Girls Love Thugs 1-5
Falling for a Hood King 1-4
Married to a Distinguished Thug 1-3
She's Gotta Have It 1-2
Me & My Dope Boy 1-3
Yazir & Nina 1-3
Forbidden Love with a Thug 1-3
You Needed Me 1-3
Shorty is in Love with a Real One 1-4
I Got Your Back 1-2
My Baby Is a West Coast King 1-4
Our Love Is the Realest 1-3
She Got It Bad for a Heartless Gangsta 1-4
She Got It Bad for a Heartless Gangsta: An AK Christmas
Hood Boyz Fall In Love Too 1-3
Nobody Can Love You Like Them Roughnecks Do 1-4
She Gave Her All to the Hood's Finest 1-5

Visit www.theshvonnelatrice.com for paperbacks!

facebook.com/ShvonneLatrice

twitter.com/shvonnelatrice

instagram.com/shvonnelatrice

$14.99
ISBN 978-1-966375-03-6

# NAMIKO "NAMI" ALLEN

I exhaled heavily, as I twisted the knob on the bathroom sink. I realized the water was cut off, and I couldn't wash my hands. This was normal now that our primary source of income was no longer.

It was early June, and the summer had just started for me. I just finished my sophomore year of college at Wayne State, with a perfect 4.0. It was nothing out of the ordinary for me, because I'd always made straight A's. My studious ways are the only reason I even made it to college. Money wasn't there, but I was blessed to have gotten an academic scholarship. It took a lot of hard work, but ultimately I made it.

I plopped down on the closed toilet and dropped my head in my hands. I had no idea what my sisters and I were gonna do for money. I was starting to regret what we'd done - or what I'd done.

My father was our sole provider after our mother died a couple years back. My mother was full-blooded Japanese and the greatest mother a girl could have. My father was a full-blooded African American, and picture perfect as well, until he started to drink. He started drinking once my mother died, and he became a whole new person. He couldn't take the fact that she was dead, and the fact that we now solely depended on his paycheck alone. He started hitting my sisters and I, and he would really take it there. I can't tell you how much money I had to spend on cheap makeup, in order to not have to walk around Detroit looking like a walking billboard for abuse.

We took the beatings for a couple years, because we kept telling ourselves he would eventually shape up and become the old Calvin Allen he used to be. Not only did that not happen, but he became worse. He started telling us we needed to fulfill his needs, including the ones only my mother took care of. At first I assumed he'd just had much more to drink than he'd ever had in his life, but I soon realized he was all too serious. Scared that he would come in and violate me, I started sleeping with a knife under my pillow. If he ever came at me, I would stab him somewhere like the shoulder; somewhere just to hurt him but not kill him.

Everything went much different the night he decided to come to my room. I panicked and accidentally plunged the knife into his throat. Blood shot out all over my face, and my father shook violently until he landed on the floor. The loud thump woke my little sister, Aniku, and she burst into my room screaming at the top of her lungs. My older sister, Kiyuki, came to see what all the commotion was, and then came up with an idea for us to hide what I'd done.

We took him out to an abandoned area and burned his body until there was nothing left. We did the same thing with the knife I used, and then made sure his ashes were discarded. We all promised to never speak about the night to anyone, and just told people he up and left if they asked. Because he was a drunk, people weren't surprised that he'd 'abandoned' us. I felt a sense of relief since my father was gone, but now that the bills were piling up, I realized we did need him for something.

"Lights are out again?" Aniku asked outside the bathroom door.

Aniku was my baby sister. She was 17 years old, and all the boys liked her. She had smooth brown skin, a pretty smile, and full lips. She had big but slanted eyes like Kiyuki and I, that we inherited from my mother, and the same long, dark curly hair that we all got from our father. She reminded me of an Asian version of Chilli from TLC. She was real skinny, but still real cute.

I leaned up a little to open the door for her. "Yeah, which means no water either," I sighed.

She walked in and sat on the dirty clothes hamper across from me. "So now what? We can't shower?" She folded her arms and rolled her eyes.

"No, but I think we still have our gym memberships. We can shower there until that gets cut off," I sighed and Aniku nodded. "You have school in the morning Aniku, you should go to bed." I added.

"I can't wait to go college, y'all get out a month early," she pouted.

"Yeah, but we start a month early too!" I chuckled and so did she before leaving the bathroom.

I sat there looking down at my feet for a couple seconds, before heading back to bed myself.

In the morning, the three of us headed to 24 Hour Fitness, to take our showers. When I got out, I stood in the mirror they had there, in my towel, and stared at myself for a couple seconds. My dark caramel complexion looked ashy, and my long dark hair needed a deep condition. My slim thick physique was in perfect condition, but I was in need of a pedicure. My full lips were still looking supple, and my big but slanted eyes were still my favorite feature.

My father was a handsome dark-skinned man, with beautiful honey colored eyes that he passed down to his girls. He and my mother were the prototype for love and marriage. I used to look up to their relationship the majority of my life. However, guys these days only liked me for the dumbest reasons. Reasons like, because I was "bad" or because I was a Blasian, which seemed to be a fascination amongst dudes these days. What happened to caring about my personality? I shook my head at my thoughts.

"Get dressed so we can drop Aniku off." My older sister Kiyuki walked by me. Kiyuki was beautiful. She was lighter than me, even though we had the same parents, had the same big but slanted honey eyes, and slim thick body. However, Kiyuki had bigger boobs and a bigger ass.

"Okay," I replied.

I slipped on a fresh pair of panties, and the matching bra over my B-cups. I pulled my white shirt over my head and pulled up my light blue skinny jeans. We were poor now, but while growing up with both parents, they provided us with nothing but the best. We still dressed the part, but we just weren't living it anymore. I threw my long wet hair up in a bun, and sat down on the bench to wait for Aniku. She soon walked out smiling, in a tight ass dress and sandals. I shook my head and laughed, then we followed Kiyuki out of the gym to the car.

"I wanna talk to you about something," Kiyuki smiled after Aniku got out the car.

"I got a way for us to make some money. Good money at that," she nodded and made a left turn.

"It sounds illegal, Kiyuki," I frowned.

"So what!"

"If I get caught, I can get kicked out of school!" I frowned at her like she was nuts.

"Look, it's this dude named Larry that said he could hook us up with this dude named Max. I'm sure you heard about Max, he's big shit around Detroit, and Larry says he is looking for some female workers to do some shit." She smiled and parked the car at IHOP.

"Yeah, probably to have orgies with him," I scoffed.

"It ain't nothing like that, but as fine as he is it couldn't hurt," she smirked.

"No, Kiyuki, I'm not doing that."

"Namiko, if you want water and power, you will. Now let's go eat," she said before hopping out the car.

She was right; we needed money bad. The least I could do was maybe listen to what the job was, and if I felt it was bullshit, I wouldn't do it. Yeah, that sounds like a plan.

# NAMIKO

"No. Wear something sexy," Kiyuki said peeking into my room.

"Why?" I frowned.

"Cause if all else fails, we'll get the job based on our looks," she smiled and winked at me. I smirked and shook my head, before removing the jeans I had on.

I decided on a camel colored tube top dress, and matching camel sandal stilettos. I put some chai colored gloss on, then put on some big gold hoops with the bangles to match.

"Perfect," Kiyuki smiled as she walked into my room. She had on a red dress, with red pumps. The shoes had a thin red strap around the ankle, to add that perfect amount of sexiness. Her long dark curly hair was up in a messy bun, and mine was hanging loosely.

"Aight lets go," she smiled.

"Where you guys going?" Aniku asked as she did her homework.

"A meeting. Don't wait up," Kiyuki quickly replied, and grabbed my wrist to rush out the door.

We pulled up to a strip club called Red Sugar, and valet parked.

"Wait, I ain't being no stripper," I said to Kiyuki.

"Girl hush! We ain't being no strippers. This is where Larry told me to meet Max. He owns this place," she replied as she touched up her makeup in the visor mirror. I rolled my eyes because I was sure she wanted to fuck this Max cat.

"K. Come on, we want to be early," she said popping her lips and getting out.

I took a deep breath, and reminded myself that this was just a meeting. Kiyuki let the bouncer know we were here to meet Max, and he radioed the info in. After receiving the okay, he opened the front door for us.

"Thank you," we said in unison.

The music in the club was so loud, that I felt the bass thumping in my chest. "Trap Luv" by Fetty Wap played as everybody danced wildly. There were girls everywhere, and they were acting as if they weren't half or fully naked.

"Welcome ladies," one of the strippers winked. I just smiled and looked away.

A guy jogged over to us and hugged Kiyuki. I'm guessing this was Larry. He was an okay looking guy, definitely nothing to write home about.

"Namiko, this is Larry," my sister cheesed.

"Nice to meet you," I nodded and smiled.

"Damn! Both of you guys are fine. Ain't nothing like a bad ass Blasian." Larry bit his lip making me roll my eyes.

Niggas like him made me hate being black and Japanese. It was like we were a type of meat that people always wanted to try out. I shook my head at my sister when he turned his back to us, and she chuckled.

We followed him down a long hallway that had velvet walls. We made a left, and then went up a winding staircase with a gold rail. Once we reached the top, we followed Larry and stopped at chestnut wooden double doors.

"You guys ready?" he smiled. Kiyuki nodded and I stayed silent.

I wasn't nervous before, but now I was. Who was this Max guy? Kiyuki said he was only twenty-three, but I was imagining some short, fat, black, old ass mob boss. Larry opened the door and told us to have a seat.

"Max will be in here in a minute. You guys want something to drink?"

"Yes," Kiyuki replied and I shook my head yes. "You drinking?" Kiyuki whispered with a surprised look.

"I'm nervous," I mouthed and she chuckled.

"Aight, we got Gin, Hennessy, Grey Goose-"

"Two Hennessey's with apple juice please," Kiyuki spoke up, ordering for us both. Larry nodded and made our drinks, then brought them over. I sipped mine, and felt like my lungs and heart were on fire.

As I sat on the couch, I looked around the nice office. Whoever this Max was, he had impeccable taste.

"Nah, you good," I heard a voice say outside the office door.

I sat up straighter and smoothed down my dress. The voice sounded like it belonged to a 23-year-old, so that was good.

"Relax," Kiyuki said bucking her eyes, and Larry laughed at me.

It seemed as if someone had turned the slow motion setting on, as I watched the doorknob twist, and then slowly open. I cleared my throat waiting to see the guy I was so scared to meet. He walked in and flashed the prettiest set of white teeth I had ever seen on a person. He had a deep honey complexion like me, appeared to be about 6'3, chocolate eyes, and full sexy lips. He wore light blue jeans, that weren't too tight or too baggy, a white Nike shirt, a red Snapback, and the Jordan retro 1's.

"Hi ladies, sorry I'm late."

"It's okay," we both said in unison. He walked past me to sit at his desk, and his cologne made him even sexier. Got damn y'all.

"So are you guys familiar with me at all?" He smiled and touched his chest, which I assumed was perfectly chiseled. I shook my head no, and he bucked his eyes and laughed.

"I mean, yes. Yes, I'm familiar with who you are," I almost stuttered.

"Oh aight," he smiled. "Relax ma, I only bite if you tell me to." He winked and I thought I would faint. Everyone else chuckled, realizing it was a joke, so I finally joined in. "Aight, so basically the deal is, the authorities were pretty hot on the guys I'd been using to do drops. They got too comfortable and slipped up. I won't say what happened to them, but take a wild guess. Anyway, I feel like I need to use females for this because, one, y'all won't attract their attention, and two, because y'all seem to be more careful." Max started the "interview".

He seemed so smart, and so sophisticated to only be twenty-three. "So what you do basically, is meet at the location I tell you, exchange the product, collect my money, and get it to me. Just 'cause you are women does not mean that the consequences will be any different if you fuck up. Is that clear?" He raised a brow, and my sister and I nodded. He stroked his very small chin hair, and checked his phone that had just chimed. "Any questions?" he asked, and we shook our heads no. "Aight cool. The first drops I give you guys will be around here and Flint only. I don't feel safe sending y'all out the area, plus I have people for that. The police I'm worried about are in Detroit and Flint. Those areas are bait," he nodded. "The first drop will be this Thursday," he said and looked at us to see if we had a problem with that.

"Sounds like a plan boss," Kiyuki smiled and licked her lips.

"Okay, so go ahead and enjoy yourselves downstairs. Everything is on the house tonight, so don't hesitate to turn up." He laughed and I stared at him with a serious expression, mesmerized by his beautiful face. I'd never been in the presence of someone so alluring.

"Oh thank you, but we're gonna go home. I need to register for next semester. Maybe another time," I smiled.

He was about to speak, but Kiyuki cut in. "She's just joking. We'd be happy to have a good time tonight," she smiled and walked to the door. I shook my head and followed behind her.

"Aye Namiko!" Max said tugging my arm lightly. I closed my eyes and enjoyed his cologne before turning around.

"Yes?" I asked, slowly pulling my arm from him.

"How old are you?" he questioned.

"I'm nineteen," I said tossing my hair to the other side uncomfortably.

"You got a boyfriend?" he quizzed, catching me off guard.

"No," I replied shaking my head.

"Good." He smiled and licked his lips, then walked back to his desk.

I half smiled, and closed his office door. Maybe this wasn't gonna be so bad. All we were doing was exchanging stuff. I shrugged and went to join my sister down in the club.

# NAMIKO

A COUPLE DAYS LATER...

Today was the first day on the job, and I was scared shitless. I kept thinking I was gonna get shot or something. I'd heard of people getting robbed during exchanges and stuff, and I did not want to end up as a casualty.

"You ready?" Kiyuki asked peeking into my room.

"Yeah, I guess," I shrugged.

"Girl, I need you to have some more confidence if you rolling with me," she spat.

"I'm good Kiyuki!" I frowned. I went into Aniku's room and hugged her tightly as hell before leaving.

"You are so dramatic Nami," Kiyuki chuckled as we walked out to the car.

"Aight, so we have to go meet with Max first," she smiled to herself.

"You like him don't you?" I smirked.

"Maybe," she replied.

"Like him as in you tryna get cuffed?" I inquired.

"Yeah girl. Or at least just have his baby. I need a shoe in on his cash flow."

"You would have his baby when he's not even with you? Just for money?" I chuckled.

"Yep! And he'd be footing the bill for my lifestyle the whole eighteen years too," Kiyuki chuckled. I shook my head at her because we were so different at times.

We got to Red Sugar and headed inside to meet with Max. I didn't even know what we were meeting him for; I just followed Kiyuki's lead.

"Hello ladies," Max said as we walked into his office.

"Hey sexy," Kiyuki smiled and waved seductively.

"Max is fine," he replied. *That was embarrassing,* I thought. "Aight, so the two bags are over there. The meeting spot and the person to meet are all in this folder," Max said handing the folders to us. "This should be quick and easy ladies. Soon as you're done, bring the money back here and I will meet you down stairs around back. Cool?" he said looking at us.

Max was way too fine, man. It was almost hard to look at him, but you couldn't help but look. I nodded nervously and Kiyuki laughed. Max got up from behind his desk and walked over to me.

"Don't be nervous," he smiled. I inhaled his cologne like I needed it to breathe.

"I'm not nervous," I lied.

"Okay good." He half-smiled and bit his lip.

"Okay, come on Nami," Kiyuki said interrupting the moment I was having with Max.

I didn't want to like him, but I think I definitely did. He was way out of my league though, and I knew we would never be. He was a boss, and I was... I was just Namiko Allen.

We grabbed the bags and headed out the back entrance. We put the address into the GPS of the truck that Max had us drive, and drove to the location. It took about an hour for us to finally get there. I pulled out the dummy phone, and handed it to Kiyuki to text the guy that was picking it up. After about five minutes, a black Cadillac pulled up, and a white man with barely any hair left exited the car. We both hopped out and he smiled at us.

"Wow, I didn't know such beautiful ladies would be coming. I would've dressed up," he snickered, and Kiyuki and I shot him a fake smile.

We did the exchange after both parties checked to make sure everything was there. Once we were in the car and on the road, I let out a sigh of relief knowing it was done.

"Fuck," I smiled.

"Easy right?" Kiyuki grinned as she pulled into the back of Red Sugar. She pulled out her iPhone and texted Max.

"You have his number?" I asked slightly jealous.

"Yeah, got it out of Larry's phone," she winked, and I shook my head.

Max and his best friend, Deshawn, appeared out the back of the club, and headed over to us to collect the bags of money. We handed them over to them, and then followed the guys back up the stairs. Kiyuki and I walked into his office, and sat down on the plush couch.

"Y'all did good," Max smiled after he and Deshawn counted the money. He handed us each $15,000, and I was caught off guard.

"We get all this just for that?" I frowned.

"Yup," Deshawn smiled.

"Next exchange is in two days," Max said before we stood up to leave.

"Okay," I replied.

I was still nervous because this next one could be the one that I die doing, or even worse- get arrested.

"Aye, you good?" Max neared me and lifted my chin.

"Yeah, I'm okay," I lied.

I was hoping he kissed my lips, but I knew that was not gonna happen. I turned to walk away and he grabbed my hand. He inter-twined our fingers and looked into my eyes.

"No need to be scared ma, I got you. Long as you stick to this side of things you'll be safe," he said, holding my hand tightly.

My palms started to sweat profusely, but I held tightly onto his hand regardless. That one little sentence made me feel so much better.

"Come on Namiko, we got a busy day tomorrow," Kiyuki said snapping me out of my trance. *What busy day?* I wanted to ask.

"Okay. Goodnight you guys." I half-smiled and stared at Max a little longer before leaving.

"Stop flirting with Max," Kiyuki said once we got into her car.

"I'm not flirting with him," I replied.

"It sure seems like it," she smiled. I relaxed a little, when I realized that she wasn't bothered.

"No, he was just trying to make me feel better," I said.

"I know. But no matter how much he flirts, don't flirt back," she said.

"Okay."

"He's the player type Nami. He will hurt you," she added.

"I know," I repeated in a more somber tone.

# NAMIKO

Tonight was my birthday, but I had absolutely nothing to do. My sisters were gone somewhere, and weren't even answering their phones. I decided to go ahead and just watch some movies until I passed out. It didn't really matter because to me, your 20th wasn't any type of milestone.

Halfway through the movie, there was a knock at the door. I was a little scared because I thought the police was always after me. I kept thinking it would be for murdering my own father, or because I was frequently transporting illegal drugs.

"Who is it?" I yelled out.

"Evelyn!" my best friend yelled through the door. I smiled because whenever she came over we always had a good time.

"What you doing here?" I beamed as she walked in.

"What? It's your birthday. Get dressed. We're going out," she said sitting down. She already had on a tight nude dress and the heels to match.

"Where at?" I smiled.

"It's a surprise! Get dressed!" she said as she pulled a bottle of Patrón out of her big bag. She had clearly already stopped by the party store.

She went to the kitchen to grab some shot glasses, as I went to get dressed. I threw on a tight canary yellow dress, with matching yellow stilettos. I wasn't into makeup so I didn't need to do that part. I combed my long black hair down, and just put some mascara on my eyelashes.

"Look at the Blasian baddie!" Evelyn chuckled. "Here," she said handing me a double shot glass.

"Why'd you get double-shot cups?" I frowned.

"Don't matter. Turn it up," she smiled. I took the shot, and then jumped around a little 'cause it burned.

"You're so dramatic," Evelyn laughed and playfully rolled her eyes.

After making me take a couple more shots, we headed out the house.

"Where are you taking me?" I smiled.

"Just let me drive please." She smiled and shook her head. I shrugged, and didn't ask any more questions for the rest of the drive.

We pulled up at some venue, but it looked like a private party. I wanted to ask about it, but I decided to just see what was going on. We got out and walked up to the front of the all-white tent like building, and the buff guy allowed us to walk inside. You could hear "Big Rings" by Future and Drake from the outside, so it was even louder once we were inside. It was dark as hell, so I decided to go ahead and start inquiring. I was just about to open my mouth, when a light came on and everybody jumped out yelling "Surprise!" I was so damn shocked. Why were they in the dark with the music blasting? Lol. I spotted my sisters who ran up to me to hug me as my mouth stayed ajar.

"Happy birthday beautiful," Max smiled and hugged me. He had his arms tightly wrapped around my waist, and my body started to tingle.

I walked over to a seating area, to relax and have some drinks. I didn't know half the people here, but I didn't care.

"Who do I thank for this?" I yelled to Evelyn over the music.

"Mr. Davis over there. He found out it was your birthday and put this together," she replied. I was shocked to hear that.

Just as she said that, he came to sit next to me in the sectioned off seating area. I tried to play it cool, by swaying and sipping my drink. I pretended not to see him; since the club was dark with only a simple blue tint, I was sure to pull it off. His cologne smelled so good as he sat down next to me. I couldn't help myself, and I turned to look at him.

"Thanks for the party," I grinned.

"You're very welcome," he smiled.

"You didn't have to do this," I said.

"Yeah I know. But I wanted to."

"Why?" I asked. He didn't respond, as he just stared at me. "What you looking at?" I chuckled.

"You. I like what I see," he cheesed, and I wanted to lick his beautiful teeth. But then, I thought about when Kiyuki said not to flirt with him.

"Thank you," I replied dryly.

He scooted closer to me, and draped his arm around my back. My breathing became heavy, and I felt like I had a ton of iron sitting on my chest.

"What?" I asked nervously.

"So, no boyfriend right?" he asked to make sure.

"No. You have a girlfriend?" I asked.

"I sure don't," he replied.

"You have a lot of girls though, I'm sure," I said. I was so nervous right now it was crazy.

"How you figure?" he asked looking dead into my eyes.

"C-cause I know you're a player," I said.

"You know nothing about me," he smiled; I loved his smile.

"I don't want to either. I'm not your type."

"What's my type?" he asked and I shrugged. I felt so dumb right now. He burst into laughter and nodded his head. "You're funny. I like that. You're sexy too." He said the last part in a serious tone. *Relax Namiko. He's only a guy,* I told myself.

"You think I'm sexy?" I asked surprised.

"Very," he said as if he was so sure of it. "Meet me at my office tomorrow." He licked his lips at me and then got up.

"Looks like you about to make your first purchase on that V Card," Evelyn leaned over to me. I forgot she was even here, that's how into this nigga I was.

"No I'm not," I replied, not even convincing myself.

# NAMIKO

By now we'd done a couple drops, and the money was worth it. The lights and cable were cut back on, as well as our cell phones. We had a fridge full of food, and I even paid to register for school.

"What you think he needs to talk to you about?" my sister Kiyuki asked as she stood in my doorway. I shrugged as I buttoned my jeans.

"I don't know. I hope I didn't mess nothing up."

"Hell no you didn't. He would've been said something. Maybe he wants to get you alone for another reason," she said as if she was thinking. I paused for a second because that hadn't even crossed my mind.

"He better not be trying to get no pussy," I frowned, and pulled my shirt over my head.

"You bet not do it!" Kiyuki raised her eyebrow.

"Hell no! I don't even know this nigga like that. Plus, he's our boss in a way."

"Who are you guys talking about?" Aniku asked walking in the room.

"Max Davis," I replied nonchalantly.

"Ohhhh, he's sexy," Aniku smiled and hi-fived Kiyuki.

"How do you know him Aniku?" I frowned and put my hand on my hip.

"Everybody knows Max. Why, you don't like him?" she asked.

"I didn't say I didn't like him. I said I'm not having sex with him." I rolled my eyes.

"So you *do* like him?" Kiyuki grimaced. She must've really liked his ass.

"Not like that. I like him as a boss, he's cool." I smiled and so did they. "Whatever. I will see y'all later and update you on what he wanted," I grinned and shook my head.

I headed to that same club he interviewed us at, and my mind was on one-hundred. I was wondering if he was actually calling me to meet with him because he had another agenda. *Nah, I wasn't his type,* I thought. He probably liked airheads with humongous asses, and 200,000 miles on their pussies.

I walked into the club, and it still amazed me how these chicks were so comfortable walking around in skimpy attire. I bobbed my head to "Couple Bands" by Fetty Wap as I walked through the decked out club.

I finally got to Max's office and knocked lightly. I heard someone walking up on the other side of the door, and I wiped my sweaty palms on my jeans.

"What's up ma?" Max smiled and moved out the way to let me in.

"Hi," I said in a low tone. I was nervous because he was so close to me, looking so fine, and smelling so damn good. "You wanted to see me?" I asked as I sat down on his couch.

He sat on the edge of his desk, and adjusted his Snapback. His sexy face was now more visible, and I felt like my breathing was getting heavy again.

"Yeah, I did," he replied biting his lip. "You said you ain't have a boyfriend, so I wanna take you out," he smirked. His dark caramel complexion looked so smooth and his lips ... Damn, those lips.

"Look Max, I'm not one of those girls who is gonna let you fuck on them until you meet a new bitch," I replied sternly. He burst into laughter and clapped his hands together.

"That wasn't part of the plan, but thanks for letting me know, ma," he chuckled.

"Well good," I said smiling since he was smiling.

"I do want to fuck you though. I ain't gone lie about that. But I was hoping it'd be for something like forever," he said.

"You don't even know me. How you know you would want to fuck with me like that? I could be crazy," I giggled.

"You could be. But that's why I wanna take you out first. If you seem crazy, I'll keep it pushing," he nodded.

"Where you wanna go?" I asked.

"Is that a yes?" he raised a brow.

"It depends where you trying to take me," I smirked like a shy schoolgirl.

"Is that a yes?" he asked again as he walked closer to me. My mouth seemed to dry up, and I felt if he touched me I'd faint.

"Fine. But just to let you know, I can't stay out late, and I'm not spending the night with you," I half-joked.

"Yet," he smirked.

"Yet?"

"You not gone spend the night with me yet. We gone make something beautiful Namiko, I can already tell." He bit his lip and let his eyes roam my body.

"Whatever. When we going out?" I inquired.

"Tomorrow night. I'm gone pick you up at 9pm on the dot."

"Okay," I said turning to walk away.

He grabbed my arm, and then placed both of them over his shoulders. He towered over me, and hugged me tight. I closed my eyes and enjoyed the moment, since he couldn't see my face. I had to telepathically tell my panties to stay up around my waist.

"See you tomorrow," he said pulling away and lifting my chin to look down into my eyes.

All I could do was nod, as his eyes seemed to hypnotize me. I had goals in life, I couldn't let this nigga steer me away from that.

# MAXIMILIAN "MAX" DAVIS

Namiko was definitely a prize in my book. She was beautiful no doubt, but that's not what drew me all the way in. When I offered for her to go and enjoy herself, they way she declined because she had more important shit to do, turned me on. She was about her business and nothing else; her beauty was just the cherry on top.

Over these past couple of weeks, I'd been making her and her sister meet with me just so I could see her fine ass. The more I got to know her, the more impressed I was. She and her sister were nothing alike. Kiyuki was that chick that wanted money and would do anything with anybody to make sure she got it. Namiko was the opposite; baby girl had pride and dignity.

Tonight I was taking her out to dinner. I wanted to do something more special, but like she said, I didn't know her like that. I didn't want to pull out all the stops, and she turn out to be some bitch I was no longer interested in. Also, I felt if we went somewhere nice and quiet, I would get a better chance to know her.

By the way, if you ain't already know, I'm Maximilian Davis, better known as Max. I run a beyond successful drug empire in the Detroit and Flint area here in Michigan. I started hustling when I was thirteen, after my dad was killed and my mom had to go find work. She'd been a housewife all her damn life, so when she had to go out and work, it was either retail or fast food places for her. She did what she had to do, but the money just wasn't enough to keep the house we'd lived in all our lives. One night, I heard my mother crying in her room because we were so broke, and I knew right then that I would need to step up and be a man.

Anyhow, my hustling and ambition got me to where I am today, ten years later. I was the king of the city, with the world at my feet. Women were a dime a dozen, and the only time they crossed my mind was when I was getting some pussy. Any other time, I was all about my business. I preferred it that way, but we all know one million hoes don't amount to one good chick. I wanted kids someday, and none of these hoes out here were worthy of being a mother to a Davis kid. That was until I met Ms. Namiko Allen.

I walked up the walkway of her house and rang the doorbell. It was a small but cozy place, and it looked like more than just she and her sisters lived here.

"Max, what you doing here?" Kiyuki asked and cocked her head to the side. Kiyuki was bad as fuck, just like Namiko, but she was a hoe fa'sho.

"Where is Namiko?" I asked.

"Right here," Namiko smiled as she emerged from the back. She was wearing a tight heather gray skirt with the matching crop top, showing her toned abs. Her dark hair was pressed and pushed behind her ears. Her big, but slanted eyes gave her an exotic appeal, and my dick was definitely taking notice.

"Damn ma. You ready?" I asked already knowing the answer. A nigga was damn near speechless.

"Yeah," she nodded. She walked out the door past me, and I watched her nice round ass.

"So can I know where we going now?" she quizzed.

"Just to dinner ma. Nosey ass," I replied and we laughed.

"I'm nosey cause I wanna know where we going?" she cheesed.

"Yep," I nodded and smiled.

"THIS IS NICE MR. DAVIS." NAMIKO BEAMED AND NODDED AS SHE looked around the restaurant Coach Insignia. "So tell me about yourself," she added.

"I'm a 23-year-old business man. I have a younger brother named Konz, and I only have one living parent," I replied.

"Is Max your real name? Or is that like an alias?" she asked.

"It's a nickname. My real name is Maximilian," I chuckled.

"I like that. Do you know what it means?" she frowned.

"The greatest," I smirked.

"No, for real. What does it mean?" she giggled.

"I'm serious ma, look it up. It means the greatest," I smiled and she laughed. Her laugh was so warm. I admired her beauty for a couple seconds before she started back talking.

"Well Maximilian, I like that," she smiled.

"So, now you tell me about yourself," I said.

"Well, I'm a 19-year-old college student at Wayne State. I study criminal justice because I want to become a forensic anthropologist. I'm the middle child of three girls, both my parents are deceased, and yes my real name is Namiko, but I don't know what it means," she finished and nodded.

"And you're a Gemini," I added as our food arrived.

"Yep, that's right. When is your birthday?" she inquired.

"November 28th," I replied. We stared at each other grinning, until she blushed and looked away. "So what the hell is a forensic anthropologist?" I asked.

"It's the person who investigates the human remains of a crime scene, in order to determine the cause of death of the victims. We spend most of our time in the labs," she nodded. *Damn, she must be smart as hell.*

"Wow Namiko, that's dope. I'm happy to see you're not the common Detroit hood rat. I think we need people like you with all this crime out here," I said shaking my head.

"I know. But I will protect you," she winked.

"Oh, you're gonna protect me?" I chuckled.

"Yeah, what's so funny?" she smiled looking as beautiful as ever. It was hard not to get lost in her smile.

"Well, I think you should leave the protecting to me ma," I bit my lip.

"I guess I can do that," she nodded.

We talked some more over dinner, and then decided to head home. "I really want to respect you and take you home, but I don't want you to leave me just yet."

"I can stay out a little longer," she smiled, and so did I. So much for her saying she didn't want to stay out late with me.

We went to my office at Red Sugar, because she didn't want to come to my house. I liked all these standards she had.

"Would you like something to drink?" I asked her once we got into my office.

"Yeah, I will take a umm ...just something not too strong," she said sitting her fine ass on the couch.

"Okay, do you like Malibu rum and pineapple juice? That's for the lightweights like yourself," I joked.

"Call me what you want," she smiled and rolled her eyes.

"I'm happy to see you're not crazy," I said sitting next to her.

"I may be hiding it." She flashed a seductive smile and sipped her drink.

I scooted closer to her and kissed her full lips. She pulled away and looked into my eyes for a little bit. I went back in for the kill, and dipped my tongue in her mouth. She wrapped her arms around my neck, as I leaned her back on the couch. I ran my hands up her skirt, and once I was between her legs, she moved her face away to break our kiss.

"What's wrong?" I asked out of breath.

"Max, I'm a virgin, and I plan to stay one until I'm married," she replied looking up into my eyes.

"Oh," I said as I got off her and sat up. It was bittersweet to hear. I was happy that she wasn't a hoe out here, with thirty bodies under her belt, but damn I wanted to fuck her.

"I probably should've told you that when you asked me out. It's okay if you don't want to date me anymore. Most guys don't when they find out," she said.

I turned to look at her beautiful face, as she waited for me to speak. Her dark caramel skin was perfect, and her big yet slanted eyes were my favorite feature of hers.

"Nah, I still like you, ma," I spoke honestly. I liked that she had these standards but damn, a nigga had needs. She blushed and smiled at my response. "Just one question. Can we have any type of sex?" I asked with a tone of hope.

"Only kissing," she replied and frowned like she'd just given me some bad news. I could tell she was holding her breath to see what I was gonna say.

"Well come here then," I said pulling her onto my lap. I dipped my tongue into her mouth, and sucked her lips for a cool little minute.

# NAMIKO

3 Weeks Later

I was surprised that Max was still interested in me, since revealing to him my sexual status. He was still taking me out at least twice a week, and didn't even try to have sex with me. However, he would kiss me for hours it seemed.

I hated having to tell guys I was one of those girls that didn't give it up, because they would always act like it was cool, and then I would never hear from them again. I thought Max was gonna do the same thing, but I guess he was actually cool with waiting on me; if we made it that far.

I was starting to really like him, and I wasn't sure if that was a good thing. I knew what he did for a living, and I knew he had lots of women. I had no interest in dealing with side hoes and jail visits, but none of that seemed to matter when I was in his presence. He was so smart and sophisticated, which was not what I expected from a guy his age and in that profession.

"So is Max your boyfriend?" my little sister Aniku asked.

"No," I replied.

"You sure? Y'all spend a lot of time together, and you talk to him on the phone every night," she raised a brow.

"He never asked me to be his girlfriend though," I replied and she laughed.

"No one asks anymore Namiko. You just kind of know," she giggled.

"Well excuse me if I'm not up on game. I haven't had a boyfriend for two years, and at that time, we asked." I cocked my head to the side and she laughed at me.

"Where you going?" Kiyuki quizzed as she stood in my doorway.

"I was gonna go to Max's house," I replied.

"Damn, you going to his house now? Finally giving it up Namiko?" She glared at me. I hated discussing Max around her.

"No, we're just gonna chill and watch movies," I blushed.

"That's how it's gonna start, and then next thing you know..." she raised her brow.

"Well maybe that's how y'all two hoes work, but not me," I joked and grabbed my purse. "He's outside. Bye," I added after reading his text.

As soon as I got into his car, he leaned his sexy self over and I kissed his lips.

"Damn," he said shaking his head, and then pulling off.

We pulled up to his house, and it looked to be about three stories. I was amazed, even though the house my sisters and I lived in was a nice size as well. That's only because it was our parents' home, obviously.

"This is nice Max. You live here alone?" I asked.

"Yeah, I do for now," he smirked, and I shook my head at him.

"So what do you want to watch?" I asked as he put Netflix on his TV.

"What are you in the mood for?" he asked removing his hat. He was so fine it should've been illegal. "Namiko," he said snapping me out of my one sided staring competition.

"Oh uh-"

"Damn ma, I know I'm a good looking guy but shit," he laughed, and I was so embarrassed.

"Whatever. I was actually thinking that you needed a new barber,"

I spat back, and we both laughed because we knew his fresh fade was perfect.

"Sure," he replied smirking.

We barely even watched the movie, because we were kissing so hard. He cut the lamp off and pulled me onto his lap. I had on a skirt and was straddling him, so I could feel his dick. It was hard as a brick, and pressing against my panties. He pulled me closer to him, to the point where I felt like it would rip through my underwear. He ran his hands up my skirt, and squeezed my ass hard. I would've stopped him usually, but his strong hands felt good all over my small body.

"Shit Nami," he moaned and sucked my lips. He reached down and felt on my pussy through my panties. "You wet as hell," he smiled.

I didn't say anything, because I didn't know what to say. He bit his lip, as he eyed my body lustfully.

"Can I see it?" he asked.

"See what?" I questioned in a low tone.

"This," he said massaging my vagina. It felt so good, but I knew it was wrong. I moved his hand away and he smiled.

"See it for what?" I finally asked.

"I wanna see how pretty it is," he responded biting his lip, and letting his hands roam my body. I paused and thought about what he was asking.

"You can see it if you become my husband. I want my husband to be the first to see anything," I finally replied in a serious tone.

"How you know I ain't gone be your husband one day?" he inquired, still holding my waist.

"Maybe you will be, but until then..." I shrugged and got off his lap.

"Fair enough," he nodded and exhaled.

"Max, I told you that you don't have to do this. I won't be mad," I said.

I *would* be mad *and* hurt honestly. I was starting to like him a lot. He was nothing like any of the other guys I met or dealt with before.

"And I told you that I can wait."

"What if we don't even make it? You would've wasted your time," I replied in a somber tone.

"This time I'm spending with you, Namiko, is not only in hopes that I will fuck. I want to spend time with you because I enjoy your company. If I never get it, I won't see it as time wasted. Now that's not to say that the nigga you do marry won't have beef with me," he joked.

The more he talked, the more I liked him. He was so honest and genuine. Not to mention the finest specimen I'd ever laid eyes on.

"You really like hanging out with me?" I asked smiling.

"Yeah I do. You know how to have a conversation. Most pretty girls are a box of rocks, but not you. That's why I call you every night; for good conversation, not for points to get in your panties, ma," he said staring into my eyes.

I didn't know if this was game he was spitting or not, but it was working. Then again, Max didn't rub me as the type to spit game. If he only wanted a fuck buddy, he seemed like the type to come out and say it. Maybe I should do it, I really liked him, and even if we didn't work out, I wouldn't regret him being my first.

"Maybe we *can* do it," I finally said, straddling him again.

"Nah, don't let me change your mind," he said.

"Oh," I replied embarrassed and looked away.

"It isn't even like that Namiko. Trust me, I want to fuck you all night long, but I want it when you want it," he said turning my face to look at him. "It's gonna be so much better for me, knowing that you really want it and not just doing it to keep me," he added.

Where the hell did he come from? I feel like he was the only guy in Michigan with a brain. God may have been rewarding me for keeping my legs closed until marriage, and I definitely liked the prize. I wrapped my arms around his neck, and we kissed until we couldn't anymore.

# MAXIMILIAN

3 Months Later

"What you been up to?" I asked my younger brother Konstantine aka Konz.

"Shit, chilling," he shrugged.

Konz was the laziest nigga on this earth. He didn't want to work, no matter how easy the job. His days consisted of watching TV, playing video games, and then spending his nights in my strip club, throwing money he didn't have at hoes.

Before my father was killed, he was a hard ass worker. My father worked three damn jobs, and never missed a day at one of them. We never wanted for anything while he was alive, and I loved him for that.

I sometimes wondered if maybe Konz had a different dad, because he couldn't have been my father's child. I guess sometimes you just get that random kid that's nothing like his parents.

My father would be so disappointed to know he had a son out here that was living like a kept bitch. I paid all his bills, and gave him spending money here and there. I tried to chalk it up to him being only twenty-one, but when I was his age, I had been moved out and was supporting myself. Yeah most of my money came from drugs, but

30

at least it was my own. As long as my mother didn't have to lift a finger anymore, I was satisfied.

"I'm gone cut yo' lazy ass off," I scoffed and shook my head.

"Why? I told you I thought of a hustle, I just need some time," he frowned.

"And what is the hustle? I've asked you several times. Maybe I can help," I replied.

"I don't want your damn help with that! I don't need you constantly reminding me that you helped me with this too," he turned his lip up then sipped his beer.

I never threw up in his face the fact that I paid his way through life, so I had no idea what he was talking about.

"When have I ever thrown anything in your face Konz?" I frowned in confusion.

"Anyway, I just need a couple months, and then I won't need your damn money anymore," he scoffed.

"Aight man," I responded defeated.

"So what's up with you and that Blasian shorty?" he had the nerve to ask in a happy tone.

"That's mine," I grinned.

"What? She yo' girl already?" he smiled.

"What you mean already? We been spending time together for the past three months." I shook my head in confusion.

"I mean, we ain't the settling down type, so I'm just amazed right now. Her pussy must be off the charts." He laughed so hard he started to choke on his beer. Dumb ass.

"I wouldn't know," I replied and waited for the jokes to fly.

"Wait, hold up. You claiming her and you haven't hit? What if the pussy is whack?" He smiled big because for some reason he was amused.

"What up doe?" My best friend Deshawn walked in.

"What's up my nigga?" I replied standing and dapping him up. He was with his little brother, Robbie and sister, Cori.

"Hi Max," Cori smiled and waved seductively.

Cori was sexy as hell, and I used to fuck her all the damn time. I liked her when I first saw her, but she was boring and had a weird laugh. It was the laugh of a serial killer, or somebody that's crazy. You know how them evil villains laugh in them cartoons? Like that. The pussy wasn't good enough for me to stick around with a chick that couldn't hold a conversation and had a scary ass laugh, so I quit her. I wouldn't say I was a player, but when I was single, I was single as fuck.

"What up Cori?" I nodded my head up.

"Aye Deshawn, talk to your best friend man. He out here claiming a chick he ain't even hit yet!" my brother Konz laughed.

Cori shot me a look, and I just shook my head and exhaled. I don't know why I tell Konz anything. Not that I was trying to hide anything from Cori, but I didn't need her mad scientist laugh having ass in my business. Cori was that chick that would follow your girlfriend on Instagram and comment little shit under y'all pictures, to hint at the fact that she fucked around with you. I hated messy hoes like that.

"It ain't always about the pussy Konz. At least he ain't out here with hoes like yo' ass," Deshawn replied.

"The hoes is where it's at. Ain't nothing like some guaranteed pussy," Konz laughed as he lit up a blunt. This nigga.

"Who are y'all talking about?" Cori finally asked.

"Some little Blasian chick named Nantucket or some shit," Konz laughed, and so did everyone else.

"Aight, so what we not gone do is be disrespectful. Her name is Namiko, and if you can't pronounce it, don't come around until you can," I spat.

"Damn bro, I can only imagine how she gone have you acting once you *do* the get the pussy!" Konz joked. "Anyway Cori, my brother here is dating a lovely, beautiful girl named Na-mi-ko. She one of them 'wait until marriage' chicks," Konz said to Cori and blew out smoke.

"I applaud you, homie, 'cause I don't think I could wait," Deshawn's brother Robbie chimed in, making Cori and Konz laugh.

"Like Deshawn said, everything ain't about getting pussy. What about being able to talk to one another? Bitches are boring these days," I said looking at a laughing Cori. She rolled her eyes and turned away. "Cori, Robbie, and Konz, can you excuse us?" I asked, ready to discuss business with Deshawn since Larry had arrived.

"Why the fuck I can't stay?" Konz frowned. He reminded me of O-Dawg from *Menace II Society*.

"Unless you gone get down, you got to get the fuck out!" I yelled. I was tired of his ass. He smacked his lips and followed Robbie and Cori out the door. "Aight y'all, our guy from Chile has agreed to relocate. I told him that we should only be getting product from him personally, because I didn't trust all these random niggas he was sending. He wasn't with it at first, but when I told him I would get my shit else-where, he agreed. So from now on, he's responsible for getting it from Chile to his home here in Michigan. All we have to do now is pick it up at his crib. No more trying to meet up at the right area, at the right time, all that shit is on him. And all the money we bringing him, that's the least he could do," I finished.

"Hell yeah, that's gone be so much fucking easier, and we will have the shit ready right after pickup damn near," Deshawn nodded.

"Exactly homie," I smiled. Business seemed to get better as time went on, and money just kept stacking.

# NAMIKO

1 Month Later

"Good morning Ms. Allen," I heard a voice say. I wiped my eyes and saw a woman standing in my room, with a tray of breakfast.

"Who are you?" I frowned.

"My name is Sonya, and Mr. Davis sent me to make breakfast for you." She smiled and brought the waffles, omelet, orange juice, and breakfast potatoes over to me. I took a sip of the juice, since my mouth felt dry.

"Thank you Sonya," I smiled and she nodded.

"Will you be needing anything else before I go?" she asked in a chipper tone.

"No, no I'm good. Thank you," I nodded.

Once she left, I decided to open the card on the plate. *Have a good day at school babe,* it read. I smiled at the note, but then jumped when I saw Aniku standing in the doorway.

"I think he's your boyfriend for sure Nami," she smiled.

"I don't know," I replied.

"Ask him," she said.

"I can't ask him something like that!"

"Ask Namiko!" she chuckled. I wanted to know too, but I was just gonna blame it on Aniku.

**Me:** *Good morning. Thank you for the breakfast.*

**Maximilian:** *You're welcome babe.*

**Me:** *My little sister wants to know if we're in a relationship.*

"I just asked," I smiled and Aniku came and sat next to me on the bed.

**Maximilian:** *Does she? Or do YOU want to know.*

**Me:** *That's not the point lol.*

**Maximilian:** *Well word around town is that you're my girl.*

"He said I am!" I smiled and Aniku and I laughed.

"Okay, y'all are way too excited," Kiyuki rolled her eyes as she appeared in the doorway.

"Guess who's Max Davis' wifey?" Aniku quizzed Kiyuki.

"Now I really don't believe that y'all ain't never fucked," Kiyuki replied folding her arms.

"Well believe it boo. He and I have yet to have sex." I cocked my head to the side.

"We will see how long that lasts," Kiyuki replied nastily.

"Do you not like Max?" I finally asked even though I already knew why she was salty.

"I just know that he's playing you. He has a girlfriend I found out," she replied. My heart dropped into my stomach.

"When did you find this out?" Aniku asked frowning.

"Last night. I was out with some friends, and his girlfriend was all over him," she smiled. Why she was smiling, I had no idea.

"What's her name?" I asked. Was I really about to cry? I'd only been dating him for four months. Was it normal for me to be this upset?

"Cori. But just be happy you didn't let him fuck Namiko," Kiyuki replied and walked away.

I couldn't even think straight after hearing that Max had a girlfriend. I silently thanked God that I didn't lose my virginity to his ass. I was done with Max.

"Good morning to you too," my best friend Evelyn said as I got into the car.

"Oh sorry. Good morning," I replied looking out the window.

"What's wrong Nami?" she asked as she pulled off.

"You remember that guy Max I was talking to or whatever?" I started.

"Max Davis? Hell yeah I remember," she chuckled.

"Well the nigga has a girlfriend," I said shaking my head.

"Who told you that?" she frowned.

"Yuki."

"I don't know Nami, she seems like a hater," Evelyn replied.

"Kiyuki? Uh no. My sister has never been a hater. She's always looked out for me," I replied, slightly irritated. Evelyn may have been my best friend, but Kiyuki was my sister, and blood was thicker than fucking water.

"So what did he say?" she asked.

"I don't know. I ain't fucking with him no more. And to think he said I was his girl," I scoffed.

"So you not gone even ask him about it?" She frowned as she pulled into a parking space at school.

"For what? So he can lie and say it's not true?"

"I would at least let him know why I'm not fucking with him no more," Evelyn said as we got out the car.

"Well that's the difference between you and I." I smiled and she laughed.

My phone went off as we walked through the campus, and Max's name flashed across.

"Hello?" I answered dryly.

"When is class over?" he questioned.

"I don't know," I said.

"You don't know when you'll be done with school?" he asked, confused.

"Nope. Have a good day," I said hanging up the phone in his face.

He called back but I sent him to voicemail. Evelyn just shook her head at me. I didn't care though; Max could scram.

# NAMIKO

Two Weeks Later

I'd been ignoring Max for the past couple of weeks, and had no intention of ever talking to him. He called me all the time and sent texts, but I never answered or replied. However, tonight was another exchange, and we had to meet with him first like always. I wanted to find work elsewhere, but there was no job that I could have that would pay me $15,000.

Kiyuki and I were walking through Red Sugar so that we could meet in Max's office.

"That's her," Kiyuki said pointing to some chick.

"Who?" I frowned.

"Max's girl Cori," she cheesed. The girl started to walk over to us, and I didn't know what to think.

"Hi, I'm Cori," she said sticking her hand out.

"I'm Kiyuki and this is my sister Namiko."

"Nice to meet you," she chuckled and then switched off.

Out of all the people in this dark club, she chose to speak with us? She must've known her man and I had been dating. But she didn't need to worry, because Max and I were finito.

Once we walked in, I spotted Max sitting on the edge of his desk, looking sexy as hell. He wore a black Nike crewneck, black jeans, and some black Jordan retro 3's. He wasn't wearing a hat, and had a fresh fade. His dark caramel complexion, looked silky smooth as usual. Of course his cologne filled the air, smelling perfect.

"Hello ladies," he smiled. Why was he so gorgeous? Why couldn't I have him like I wanted? I didn't say hi back but Kiyuki did. He handed over the folders, and we were ready to be on our way.

"Kiyuki, can you give us a minute?" Max asked.

"No Kiyuki-"

"Namiko," he said cutting me off sternly.

I saw he was serious, so I didn't speak up any further. Once Kiyuki left and the door was closed, Max came and sat next to me.

"Why you tripping babe?" he asked like he was innocent.

"Cause you lied to me," I replied sounding like a little ass girl.

"What did I lie about?" he frowned.

"You have a girlfriend," I said feeling myself become upset again. He burst into laughter, and I just watched him with a serious facial expression.

"Who is my girlfriend? I wasn't aware that I had one," he grinned showing his perfect white teeth.

"That girl, Cori," I said.

"Ma, Cori is not my girl. Never has been," he said chuckling.

"She's not?" I asked and he shook his head no. I smiled and blushed.

He pulled me into his lap, and I dipped my tongue in his mouth. We hungrily kissed one another, as his strong hands roamed my small frame.

"Next time you hear something, come talk to me," he said in a low tone.

"I think I love you Max," I blurted out before thinking. *Shit*.

"You think?" he smiled.

"No, I do," I nodded.

"It's okay if you don't love me back. That's not why I told you," I told him honestly.

"I think I love you too Ms. Namiko," he replied staring into my eyes.

"You just saying it 'cause I said it," I smiled.

"Nah, these past couple of days that I hadn't seen or talked to you made me realize my feelings," he replied seriously.

"So I'm really your girl?" I asked as I played with his short fade.

"You've been my girl. I told you that," he said biting his lip. Damn I loved when he did that. "I can let Deshawn go with your sister tonight, and you can come home with me," he added.

"You sure?" I frowned.

"Positive," he nodded.

Once Deshawn and Kiyuki were gone, Max and I headed back to his home. I had to remind myself of my morals, so that I wouldn't give it up to him tonight. I wasn't sure how much longer I could be around him and not want to make love. I had strong feelings for him, but I knew it was something missing that would make it all complete - sex.

After watching some movies, eating food, and playing a couple video games, we retired to the bedroom.

"I don't know if I can wait much longer," I said caressing his chin hair.

We were laid in his bed, with only the TV on. He looked into my eyes, and then started to suck my lips. He kissed me hard, and positioned himself on top of me, between my legs. I only had on my bra and panties, since I denied the t-shirt he tried to give me. I wrapped my legs around him, and grinded on his hard dick, that was threatening to burst through his boxers.

"Fuck... I want you," he moaned as he kissed my shoulders. "Does oral count?" he smiled and I nodded while giggling.

"Can I ask you something?" he inquired.

"Yeah," I replied in a low tone.

"Why do you want to wait until marriage?" he quizzed.

"My parents said that only my husband should be the one to have sex with me, and I don't want to be a hoe," I replied. He was still between my legs, with his dick pressed against my silk thong panties.

"Sex doesn't make you a hoe. Your reasons for having sex are what can make you a hoe. If you just spread your legs for a man 'cause he has money, or fucking your dude's homeboys, things like that make you a hoe. Not having sex with a man you love, or are in a relationship with. And I'm not saying this to change your mind; I'm saying this so that you aren't misinformed. I will wait for you," he said stroking my hair.

I never looked at it that way, and a part of me felt like he was right.

"You think we're gonna be married?" I asked.

"Yeah, I do," he smiled and pecked my lips.

"I want you Max, but I just can't," I said sadly. I felt like he was getting tired of waiting on me. "You can have sex with someone else," I added.

"What? I'm not gonna cheat on you Namiko. I can wait." He replied.

I felt so dumb for even offering that, knowing I didn't want him sleeping with someone else. I just wanted to keep him.

"I know you wouldn't cheat. That's why I love you. You deserve to be my first," I half-smiled, while caressing his face.

"I want to taste you though," he said pulling on my panties.

"That's sex Max," I chuckled.

"Pretend it's not," he said removing my panties. *What are you doing Namiko?* I asked myself.

"Ooh." I tensed up as I felt his lips on my vagina. He sucked on my clit, and dipped his tongue in my opening. "Uuhhhh that feels good Max," I moaned. He brought his head up, and I got scared. "Don't put your fingers in me," I whined, feeling like I had to pee. It felt so good, whatever he was doing to me. Next thing I knew, liquid released from my body, and it was the best feeling in the world. Max stood up on his knees, and licked his sexy lips.

"Damn. That was good," he smiled. He ran a finger along my vagina, and I jumped. "Relax, I'm not gone stick my fingers in you," he chuckled.

"I love you," I said out of breath.

# NAMIKO

## 2 Months Later

I was spending every waking moment with Max. I felt bad, because I was barely doing the exchanges with Kiyuki, and I knew it was bothering her. I think she still liked Max, and I felt like I betrayed her by dating him.

"Wow, you're home?" Kiyuki asked as she walked into my room.

"What do you mean?" I asked even though I already knew the answer.

"You seem to always be running behind Max," she spat.

"I don't run behind anybody; we hang out a lot. That's my boyfriend," I frowned.

"After I told you that I liked him," she said shaking her head.

"You told me you wanted him, just so you could pin a baby on him Kiyuki. Don't pretend like you had a real crush," I replied sitting up in my bed.

"And I told you he had a girlfriend," she glared at me.

"No he doesn't," I quickly shut her down.

"Is that what he told you? You're so naive sometimes, Namiko. You believe everything that nigga tells you." She shook her head and scoffed.

"No I don't," I replied, wondering if I really did just believe everything he told me without thinking first.

"Did you ever ask why she was all over him at the club the night I saw them?" She raised a brow and I shook my head no. "See, you too inexperienced in the relationship department to be with a nigga like Max. He knows that, and that's the only reason he even likes you," she said. I didn't say anything because I just didn't have anything to say. "I warned you months ago to not flirt with him. You don't listen. I've been around Namiko. Break it off before you find yourself in love and giving up the goods." I looked away from her and she stared at me. "You let him fuck you Namiko!" she said in a high-pitched voice.

"No, we just... well... he just ate me out," I replied in a low tone.

"You're so dumb sometimes. You love him?" she asked.

"Yeah," I nodded.

"Well at least you still got your virginity. But promise me you will stop messing with him. He's just gaming you up to be the first one in your panties."

"Okay, I promise," I lied.

I was in too deep with Max already. I wanted to be with him, and Kiyuki wasn't gonna stop that. I knew she meant well, but I also knew she liked Max. She wanted him for herself.

"Good, I guess I can count on you to actually go on this exchange with me tonight," she smiled standing up.

"Yup," I replied and half-smiled. She kissed my cheek and then left out the room.

Maybe Evelyn was right about Kiyuki being a hater. She never cared about who I dated before, but now she was so invested in keeping me away from Max. But then again, she liked him and maybe she felt hurt. Ugh! I was so confused about her intentions. One thing I wasn't confused about though, was the fact that I loved Maximilian.

It was time to head to Red Sugar to get the folders for the exchange tonight. I really wanted to just let Larry go with Kiyuki, and hang with Max all night like we'd been doing. Then again, it wasn't fair that he was still paying me the $15Gs and I wasn't even doing the work.

As soon as we walked in, Max wrapped his arms around my waist. He kissed my lips, and then I slid my tongue into his mouth. I had forgotten that Kiyuki, Deshawn, and Larry were in the office.

"You look good in your all black," Max smiled and eyed my body.

"Thank you baby," I smiled seductively and he bit his lip. I wanted him to fuck me so bad, I needed prayer and even King Jesus himself at this point.

"So Kiyuki, Larry is gone be rolling with you tonight," Max said looking at her. I saw she was bothered, so I decided to speak up.

"No Max, I can go."

"You ain't tryna chill with ya man?" he smiled.

"I am but when I get back, we can go to your house like usual," I offered.

He stared at me for a little bit, and then exhaled heavily. I spent the night with him every single night, so he knew I was really gonna come.

"Okay," he finally replied. I smiled and kissed his lips. He squeezed my ass, and I jumped and giggled.

"We're on a time crunch," Kiyuki barked. Max pecked me once more, and bit his lip as he stared at me lustfully. Ah, he was everything. I wanted to lick his smooth caramel skin, and wrap my legs around his 6'3" muscular frame.

"You promised," Kiyuki said as we got into the car.

"Kiyuki, it's not fair. We're in love," I pouted.

"No, *you're* in love! He doesn't love you, and he never will!" she scowled at me.

"Let's just go to the meeting spot," I replied buckling my seat belt.

I was not gonna leave my man just because she wanted to use him for a come up. She needed to get over it.

# MAXIMILIAN

My mom had been blowing me up all week saying she needed to talk me. I was busy as hell, but I knew I needed to make some time for my moms. It was Sunday afternoon, so I figured today would be perfect since it was the day meant for relaxation.

"Finally," my mother spat as I walked through her living room. I sat down on the couch and looked around the place.

"Ma, what happened to the maid I hired for you?" I frowned.

"Alfred didn't like her." She shook her head.

"You mean he slept with her so you fired her?" I asked already knowing the answer.

Alfred was my mother's boyfriend, and he was not worthy of her at all. I'd already fought that war of trying to make her see that, but nothing could or would change her mind about him. She asked me to let her live her life, so I did. As long as he wasn't putting his hands on her, we were good. She didn't respond to my accusation, so I decided to just get to the damn point.

"What was so important that you needed to talk Ma?"

"Well, Alfred has um, fell on some hard times."

"What the hell does that have to do with me?" I shook my head because I was confused.

"He is about to get evicted, and since you said he can't live with me, I was wondering if you could spot him some money," she finished.

She was right, if I was footing the bill for my mom's crib, Alfred's bitch ass could not stay there.

"I'm not giving no man old enough to be my damn dad some money, Ma," I stated matter-of-factly.

I couldn't even believe she was asking me this shit. She knew I hated that nigga and wouldn't dare help his ass out.

"Do this for me," she pleaded.

"No Ma, why you even like this nigga? He ain't worth shit!" I yelled.

I hated to see my mom acting like these weak ass hoes in the streets. How could she go from someone like my father, to a nigga who couldn't even pay his own damn rent. A nigga that had to have his woman ask her son for money. I may have respected him more, if he came to me himself at least.

"I love Alfred honey. I'm not gonna leave him just cause he's having a hard time," she whined.

"He's always having a fucking hard time!"

"So I'm just supposed to leave? I didn't leave your father when he was broke," she frowned.

"Firstly, don't ever compare your bum ass boyfriend to my father. Second, my dad was 19 years old when y'all were broke. This nigga is what, 50?" I frowned.

"Look, it's just $3500, that's nothing to you. He'll pay it right back, Maximilian," she begged. I hated to see her beg.

"You know damn well he not gone pay me back shit. I'll do this for you since he got you stressing like the bitch he is. But after this Ma, don't ask me to do nothing else for this nigga. He is not a man, you deserve better," I said peeling off the $3500, and handing it to her. "Did you need any money?" I asked.

"I need my hair and nails done," she smiled.

This nigga couldn't even send his woman to get her hair and nails done. I didn't mind paying for my mom's pampering, but it was all the more reason why she didn't need this nigga, Alfred. He was a bill, not a companion.

"Here you go," I said peeling off an extra 2Gs.

"Thank you baby. And when can I meet your little girlfriend?" she cheesed.

"Konz told you about her, huh?" I smirked and she nodded. "Next Sunday, the three of us can have lunch," I replied.

"Okay."

"Aight, take care Ma," I said kissing her cheek and leaving. I prayed to God my mom got rid of that nigga, because he was trifling as fuck!

I went straight to Namiko's house, so she could come spend the night with her man. It was getting harder and harder for me not to fuck her. Everything from her beautiful golden skin and honey colored eyes, to her slim thick body was perfect. I ain't even know what slim thick was, until the homie referred to Namiko as slim thick. She had a nice plump ass, medium sized perky titties, nice thighs, and a flat stomach. She was smaller than the girls in the videos, as well as the Instagram models, but it was still something to grab on. Skinny or slim thick, she was still fine as hell. I'd never dated a half Japanese chick either, but she seemed to be the same as a full-blooded black woman anyway, except the eye shape. I couldn't believe she'd gotten through life as a virgin looking like that.

"I missed you baby," Namiko said as she got into the car.

"I told you about wearing those dresses around me," I bit my lip.

"I know but I was rushing," she chuckled.

"I love yo' pretty ass," I replied licking my lips.

As soon as we walked into the house, I grabbed her from behind. I started feeling on her thighs, and slowly going up her dress.

"Stop Max," she giggled.

"I already feel bad about letting you... you know," she smiled.

"Letting me eat that pussy?" I said sucking on her neck.

"Don't say it like that," she blushed.

"Say it like what? That's what I did," I laughed and so did she. "You should let me do it again," I said, spinning her around and pecking her soft lips. I tongued her down, and sucked on her lips at the same time.

"No..." She moaned in between kisses, as I pushed her onto the stairs. "Right here?" she asked bucking her eyes as I tugged her panties off.

I didn't say anything, as I pulled her swollen clit into my mouth.

# KIYUKI ALLEN

Pissed off. Irritated. Envious. Disgusted. That's pretty much how I was feeling right now. Namiko's simple-minded ass knew I had my eyes on Max this whole damn time. She didn't even know who this nigga was. I knew he just wanted to fuck, and a part of me didn't want my little sister getting hurt. On the other hand, it was because she betrayed me. Last time I checked, when someone tells you they feeling a person, you don't go after them. I was starting to believe she wasn't a fucking virgin.

She and Aniku are the only ones who decided to listen to my parents as far as that staying a virgin shit, but me? I started fucking at age fifteen. It was just little niggas around school, but soon enough, older dudes starting looking too. I got addicted to fucking with boss niggas because their pockets were fat. Soon as you gave up the pussy, they were ready to give you some money. It was the perfect trade-off in my book.

Anyway, regardless of my sister's relationship with Max, I was coming for him. I knew he thought I was sexy, and I'm sure sitting on his dick would be no problem, especially because he wasn't getting any from Namiko.

"Where you going?" Aniku asked me.

"Out real quick," I replied putting on lipstick.

"Damn, can I come?" she frowned. "Namiko is never here anymore, and you always going out. I'm bored as hell," she whined.

"If I let you come, I need some privacy. Meaning we gonna split up until I come find you," I said pointing my finger in her face.

"Sure, whatever," she shrugged and then ran off to change clothes.

Once Aniku was dressed, we headed to Red Sugar. "Damn, this place is crazy," Aniku said with her eyes bucked, as I searched the room for the person I was here to meet.

"Go dance and shit. I will be back in about twenty minutes, okay?" I said.

"Where you going?" she questioned.

"Aniku, please," I turned my lip up.

"Fine!" she said smacking her lips and strutting off.

I made sure she was gone, and then went through the crowd of people to my new friend.

"Hey," I smiled.

"Hey Kiyuki," Cori smiled as well.

"May I?" I asked pointing to the couch.

"Please do," she continued to smile.

"So what's the status on your sister and Max?" she asked.

"She said he's her man and that they're in love. Can't no man fall in love without touching the pussy," I smirked and she laughed.

"I know that's right," she concurred and we hi-fived.

See, Cori thought I was doing this so she and Max could be together, but nope. I was doing this so Max and *I* could be together, or at least have a baby.

"Let's go see if he is upstairs," I suggested.

"K," she responded, and we headed to the back to see my man.

The door was closed, so she knocked lightly. We both waited in anticipation to see if he was in there. I finally started to smile when the door opened, and Max peeked his head around.

"What's up?" he asked.

"Let us in Max," Cori smiled seductively. He paused for a second, and then moved out the way so we could walk in. I closed his door, and locked it as Cori started to undress.

"Cori," Max said.

"Just relax babe. I know you been without." I winked and started to undress as well.

"Y'all need to lea-" Max tried to say, but just as I stepped out of my dress, there was a knock at the door.

"Shit. Who is it?" Max yelled out as I slid my dress back on, and Cori stayed half naked. "Oh, hey babe," Max said peeking out the door so the person couldn't see. I assumed it was Namiko by the way he addressed them.

"Let's go," she said sounding all happy. Yep, it was Namiko.

"Umm, aight, hold on. Go get a little drink from downstairs," he offered.

"I don't want to drink tonight. Why you peeking your head out like that? What's in there?" she inquired and Cori smiled big. Namiko attempted to get by, but Max was blocking her. "Max, is it a girl?" she asked. He didn't say anything, so Cori walked over.

"Excuse me, oops, forgot my dress," she said as she walked back over and grabbed it.

I was fully dressed by this time, hiding on the other side of the couch. Since the jig was up, Max moved from the doorway so it could fully open. I stayed hidden so that she couldn't see me.

"You had sex with her?" Namiko asked Max.

"No babe, she-"

"Never mind," she said and then quickly left out of the office.

"Namiko!" he yelled.

"Aight, come out y'all two!" Max demanded, and we did as we were told. His caramel complexion was starting to darken he was so angry. I knew we had fucked up, and it made me feel giddy as hell on the inside.

# NAMIKO

I heard Max calling after me, but I was too embarrassed to stop and talk. I knew he couldn't wait, and for some reason I was ashamed. I guess because I was really believing that he would wait for me to have sex, and I was telling everybody that would listen that he would too.

"Nami!" I heard my sister Aniku call after me.

"What are you doing here?" I frowned at her.

"I came with Kiyuki," she smiled.

"Kiyuki is here?" I quizzed and she nodded. "Oh well, are you ready to go?" I asked.

"No, I will ride home with Yuki," she cheesed.

"Okay, see you at home," I replied and walked off.

I wished I hadn't stopped to speak with my little sister, because now Max had caught up to me. I quickly rushed out, hoping I could still get away.

"Namiko! Chill!" he said grabbing my arm in the parking lot.

"Oh I didn't hear you," I lied, obviously.

"Right," he smirked.

"I can explain about what you saw up there," he started.

"It's okay Max. I don't need an explanation," I smiled.

"You not mad?" he frowned in confusion.

"No, I shouldn't have expected you to wait. We can still be friends though." I forced a smile on my face, although I wanted to cry.

"Nami..." he said scooting closer to me, and grabbing my face. I looked up into his eyes waiting for him to finish. "I didn't do anything up there. I told you I'm waiting for you," he said in a low tone.

"I don't want to force you," I said slightly above a whisper.

"Do I seem like the type to allow someone to force me to do anything?" He half smiled and I shook my head no. "Okay then. I love you Namiko Allen."

"I love you too Maximilian." I smirked at the fact that I used his full name.

He wrapped his arm around my neck and pulled me into a kiss. I wrapped my arms around his waist and hugged him tightly, with my eyes closed. It should've been illegal for another human being to make me feel this way. I felt like I was floating on air whenever his lips touched mine. I would always forget where I was, or who was in the room; it was like only he and I mattered. I was on the verge of proposing to his ass so we could make love. I needed it to happen. Would it be so bad if I just let him? Waiting until marriage was for back in the day. The modern era is so different.

"You okay?" Max inquired.

"Let's go do it Max," I said and bit my lip.

"Do what?" he asked.

"Sex. Let's have sex," I said looking up at him.

"You sure?" he questioned and I nodded.

Once we got to his home, we were kissing like maniacs. We stripped down naked, and he admired my body as I lay in the bed.

"Damn," he commented as he rubbed his hands over my naked body.

I kept taking deep breaths, because I didn't know what this was gonna be like. I imagined that we would become closer, adding that final piece to our relationship puzzle.

He removed his boxers, and my eyes locked onto his big dick. It was about ten inches long, and caramel just like him. He climbed in-between my legs, and started to suck on my nipples hard. *This is wrong*

*Namiko,* I thought. *You killed your father; you could at least keep your promise to him.*

"Max... I can't," I finally said.

"Yes you can," he said kissing my stomach.

"No, I can't. I have to wait," I said pushing his head away. He exhaled heavily and plopped next to me. "I'm sorry," I said in a low tone.

"You always sorry! One minute you want it and next you don't! Make up your mind Nami, you gone give me fucking blue balls with all this back and forth," he spat.

I paused for a second, and then decided I should leave. He was getting frustrated with me, and I couldn't blame him. I needed to just end our relationship now, before we got to a point where we couldn't even be cordial.

"Where you going?" he asked as I climbed out of the bed and grabbed my panties to put on.

"I'm gonna go home," I replied.

"Why?" he frowned, irritated.

"Cause I think we should end it Max," I said feeling tears well up.

"End it? Why the fuck should we end it? We been dating almost a damn year now, and all of a sudden you want it to be over? Nah, I need a good fucking reason for wasting my time," he exclaimed. "Wait. Nami, I didn't mean to say I wasted-"

"It's fine Max. I will see you tomorrow for the exchange." I half smiled and wiped the single tear that managed to escape my eye. He reached out for me, but I moved out the way, and out the door.

When I got home, the lights were off and everyone was asleep. I thanked God because I didn't want to answer any questions as to why I wasn't with Max. As soon as I got in my room, I locked the door, and climbed in the bed fully dressed. Max sent me a couple texts, but I didn't even read them. I cried into my pillow in order to muffle the sound, and after a couple hours, I finally fell asleep.

# MAXIMILIAN

2 Months Later

Namiko and I had been broken up for a while now. At first I was thinking maybe it was a good idea. I knew I had needs, and she couldn't fulfill them at this point. We barely even talked to one another unless it was about her work. She comes to do the exchanges with Kiyuki, and leaves right after it's done. Kiyuki stays around and clubs, but not Namiko.

I admit I wished she did, because I missed her. I was back fucking with Cori, and a couple other bitches, which made me realize that relationships really are more than just sex. I missed Nami's and my conversations, jokes, and just the time we spent with one another. I had too much pride to call or text her, and of course she didn't try to contact me at all. I really don't know why I thought I could be over a girl that I fell in love with, after a couple months, but that was what I assumed. I thought as soon as I busted my first nut since being with her, I would be good. Boy was I wrong, and wishing I could turn back time.

"She ain't your type bruh," my brother Konz shook his head.

"What is my type?" I chuckled.

"First of all, bitches that give up the pussy," he said taking the blunt from me.

"What do you even talk about with these hoes?" I laughed.

"Talk? We don't need to talk. How they gone talk with my dick in they mouth?" He smiled and we laughed.

"You a damn mess." Deshawn laughed as he blew out smoke.

"You talk to these hoes?" Konz frowned.

"Not the hoes, no, but the women I'm trying to date, yes," I replied and shook my head.

"I ain't got time for that shit," he shrugged.

I was about to speak, but my phone rang cutting me off. I saw it was Cori calling, and blew out a frustrated sigh. I knew I shouldn't have started fucking with her again, because it would get her hopes up.

"Aye y'all, I'm about to go," I said standing up to leave Konz' place.

"Can you drop me off at the crib?" Deshawn asked and I nodded.

After dropping Deshawn off, I headed over to Cori's so I could talk to her ass. "Hey daddy," Cori smiled and wrapped her arms around my neck.

"Hey ma," I replied dryly, as I lightly pushed her off me.

"You hungry? I made dinner," she smiled. Cori was gorgeous with her thick ass, but I just didn't click with her outside of the bedroom.

"Nah, I won't be long," I said pulling her to the couch.

"What's wrong babe?" she asked with a concerned look.

"Look, from here on out we just gone be friends. Not with benefits, just homies," I exhaled.

"Why? What happened? What did I do?" she frowned.

"You ain't do anything I just don't want to string you along, knowing I don't want to be with you," I replied.

"Is it because of Namiko?" she pouted.

"Nah, it has nothing to do with her. It's just, you deserve better than a guy who doesn't want anything more than sex from you," I told her.

"I don't care though Max. That could change. Just let us be together, and you will start to love me. I promise," she said with tears sitting in her eyes and waiting to fall. I was a sucker for a crying woman. "Please Max," she said scooting closer to me, and caressing my face.

"Okay ma," I finally replied and exhaled. She smiled big, and hugged me tight as hell.

This was wrong... so wrong.

# NAMIKO

"Told you," Kiyuki said walking into my room.

"Told me what?" I questioned.

She showed me her phone, which displayed a picture of Max and Cori on Instagram. It made my stomach hurt to see them together. I felt so stupid for believing all of the things he told me. Kiyuki was right the whole time, and I felt even worse for thinking that she was just jealous.

"Who cares," I said handing her the phone back.

"Why you not dressed?" she frowned.

"Cause I don't feel good," I said sitting on my bed.

"We need to get this money Nami. The mortgage needs to be paid, and you know we go half. I'm not paying it alone," she spat folding her arms.

"Just go Nami." Aniku walked into my room with a bowl of ice cream.

"I said I'm sick," I replied, rolling my eyes.

"So what, now you not gone make money 'cause of this nigga? How you gone pay for school Namiko? You gone drop out over one nigga? Get over it. Nothing even happened between you two!" Kiyuki turned her lip up in disgust.

*Something did happen between us! He made me love him!* Is what I wanted to say.

"You're right," I responded instead, and Aniku nodded in agreement.

I got dressed and prepared to see Max. I was gonna act like I didn't care, and that everything was peaches and cream. He didn't deserve to know he broke my heart. He didn't deserve all that credit.

We got to Red Sugar and like always, my nerves were on 1000. We headed back to Max's office, to get the details of our consumer as usual. My stomach felt like it was churning butter, when we walked in to see Cori on Max's lap. I wanted to go in a corner and cry, but instead I had to hold my head high, and keep my shoulders back.

"Hello," Kiyuki smiled and Cori waved to us.

"Here y'all go," Max said and slid the folders across his desk. He barely looked at us as he messaged someone on his phone. I now wanted him to see how bad he hurt me.

"Okay, we should be back in about two hours," Kiyuki said looking in the folder.

She turned to walk out, but I stayed planted for a couple seconds. I realized he wasn't gonna pay me any mind, so I followed behind my sister.

"I can't keep doing this Kiyuki," I said to my sister once we pulled onto the road.

"Over time you won't even care about him Nami," she replied dryly. I could tell she was irritated by my comments.

"I don't think so Kiyuki. I get sick seeing him with her," I said on the verge of crying.

"Grow the fuck up Namiko! Stop worrying about a nigga who probably don't even remember the time y'all spent together. Ain't like y'all had memorable sex or something," she said, laughing at the latter part of her statement and raising her brows.

"Why did you make that face?" I asked. She didn't respond, but a smile was breaking through.

"Don't be mad," she said showing all thirty-two by now.

"You had sex with Max?" I asked in a low tone. *Please say no,* I thought.

"It was a threesome with Cori. It just happened Nami. We were drinking one night, babe," she said sympathetically. "He was no good for you. Don't even worry about him," she added as tears glided down my cheeks.

"Why did you fuck him Kiyuki?" I shouted breaking down. I couldn't believe she would do that to me.

"I told you it was an accident! Plus, I told you I was interested in him first! You chose to go after him anyway. I should be mad at you Namiko!" she spat, keeping her eyes on the road.

"But I told you I loved him! You don't love him!" I cried hysterically as I stared out the front windshield.

"And clearly he don't love you if he would fuck your sister," she said nonchalantly. She was right, and I had nothing else to say.

The rest of the ride was quiet, and so was the ride back to the club. Once Max counted the money, he paid us our fee. Kiyuki walked out, and I was right behind her until Max stopped me.

"You've been crying Nami?" He frowned as he searched my eyes.

"Just stop," I said slightly above a whisper, and walked away.

I usually would go home, but I needed a drink. Since I was under age, I had to convince a guy to buy me something.

"I got you ma," some guy whose name I learned was Ronald, smiled.

"Thank you," I replied and tapped impatiently on the bar, as I waited for my Adios Amigos. I needed to get fucked up.

After drinking two of those, I was feeling free and loose. "Liquor" by Chris Brown came on, and I started to sway to the music with my eyes closed. Ronald walked up behind me, and wrapped his arms around my waist. I swayed up against him, and then started twerking my ass seductively to the beat of the song.

"Damn," he commented as I went to work. I felt so carefree and I loved it.

I spotted Kiyuki watching me from afar and smiling. Ronald turned me to face him, and then dipped his tongue in my mouth as Chris sang *All I want is yooou*. All I could think about is how bad I wanted Maximilian. I was too over the edge to care that Ronald was a complete stranger, so I reciprocated his kiss.

"Come home with me," he whispered into my already hot ear.

"Okay," I slurred and smiled. He draped his arm over my shoulder, and pecked my lips before we headed out looking like a couple.

On our way out, I spotted Max at the doorway talking to a doorman. "Where you headed Namiko?" he asked as he eyed Ronald.

"You don't worry about that partner," Ronald responded, and proceeded to walk with his arm still around me. Max grabbed my arm roughly, and snatched me back towards him. "Aye man! The fuck you doing?" Ronald yelled.

"Get the fuck out of my club!" Max yelled.

"Just wait outside for me," I cheesed at Ronald. He smirked back, and then nodded. "What you want?" I frowned turning my attention back to Maximilian.

"So you leaving the club with random niggas now?" he asked.

"Yep," I smiled.

"Damn, are you even a virgin still?" he quizzed.

"I sure ain't," I lied.

"Who you fuck Nami?" he asked through gritted teeth. Damn, he was angry as fuck.

"Some guy from school." I shrugged and stared up into his eyes.

"Wow," he chuckled and nodded.

"Sorry you wasted your time for nothing." I cocked my head to the side.

"Looks like I dodged a bullet 'cause I see you a hoe," he shrugged. Tears welled up in my eyes, but I wiped them before they could fall.

"Are we done here?" I asked trying to cover my sadness with an attitude.

"We are most definitely done here," he said smiling and walking away. I wanted to stop him and tell him I was lying, but I couldn't.

I walked out to the parking lot, and saw Ronald all hugged up on some other bitch. I plopped down on the sidewalk, and dropped my head into my lap.

"Nina!" Ronald called out. Although that wasn't my name, I picked my head up and looked to the right at him. "You coming with us?" he asked. I shook my head no, and waved him off. He shrugged and got into the car with the mystery girl.

After watching a few cars drive by, I decided to call a taxi and go home. With the night of killing my father being in first place, tonight was the second worst night of my life.

# MAXIMILIAN

One Month Later

"Don't you think we should be more serious Max?" Cori asked as she stood in the doorway of the bathroom.

"More serious as in?" I asked while turning the shower on. We just fucked for hours, and all I wanted was a hot shower and a good night's sleep.

"I don't know. I wanna get married," she said. Was she crazy? I knew hooking back up was a dumb ass idea on my part.

"Cori, we not there yet ma," I replied.

"When are we gonna get there?" she inquired.

"I don't know. All I know is that right now, marriage is not even on the table," I exhaled.

"What will it take for marriage to get on the table?" she asked folding her arms. "I been fucking you on and off for three years Max!"

"Yes. Exactly. You've been fucking me and nothing else. Marriage is 50% fucking and 50% love Cori, and right now we stuck at 50% fucking," I said getting in the shower to wash off. "Leave me alone. Shit!" I shouted over the sound of the water.

She stood there staring at me for a little bit, and then walked out of the bathroom. These women killed me man. I was thinking about just breaking up with Cori and being single. She was stressing me out way too fucking much. All she did was nag about moving forward, and our relationship seemed to be forever stagnant.

After my shower, I wrapped my towel around my waist, and went to the bedroom to change. Namiko still crossed my mind every now and then, but I was a little salty that she had given up her body to some random nigga from school. I was with her for almost a year and she runs off and fucks some dude from school? Cool. I wanted to kill whoever he was, but shit, it wasn't his fault he got the cookies first.

I slammed my dresser drawer at the thought. I wanted to be the first nigga to touch her intimately. I loved her ass, and I felt like her virginity was mine. Something that we were supposed to share as two people in love, she gave to some random Joe Blow. Whatever though, she was probably gone be hoeing around Michigan now anyway.

I wish I didn't have to see her all the time. She was still doing the exchanges for me, but we didn't talk to one another. You would never even know that we were once in love.

"What's wrong baby?" Cori walked behind me and reached up to massage my shoulders. I threw her hands off me, and she stared at me concerned.

"I'm sorry ma, I ain't mean to push you," I replied and exhaled. I walked past her, and got in the bed so I could rest my nerves.

"These are the folders. Namiko, you go on this one alone, I have a separate one for Kiyuki," I said sternly.

"Alone? I don't want to go alone," she whined.

"I didn't ask what you wanted to do," I said.

"What if something goes wrong?" she asked.

"You better hope it doesn't for your sake," I replied coldly.

"Max, please," she pleaded as her beautiful honey eyes became glazed over. I still loved this girl I was starting to see.

"Grow some balls Namiko. Go on this one alone, or I'm firing you," I spat.

She paused and then took the folder from me. She looked over the contents, and then left out my office to do the exchange. Was I being mean on purpose? You damn right I was. I loved her ass and she ran off and gave a nigga something that belonged to me. I was getting angry just thinking about it.

"You good Max?" Deshawn asked.

"I'm great, why?"

"You were kind of mean to Namiko," he frowned.

"I wasn't being mean, I was being stern. If she wants to work for me she needs to do the job without any questions," I said looking in one of my drawers.

"Damn, she got yo' ass," he chuckled.

"What?" I asked shooting daggers at him.

"You in love nigga. I ain't never seen you sweat like this over a bitch. She got you mad as hell," he laughed.

"Ain't nobody mad! I don't give a fuck about Namiko, and I never have nor will I ever," I said and looked up from my drawer to see her in the doorway.

"I had a question but never mind..." Her sentence trailed off and she turned to leave.

"Nami!" I called out. I did not want her to hear what the fuck I just said. Not because it would hurt her feelings, but because it wasn't true at all. "Nami!" I yelled running after her through the club. By the time I got outside to the back lot, she was pulling out in the truck. "Damnit!" I said punching the air as I turned around to walk back inside. "I fucked up., I said in a low tone as I walked back into my office.

"That's what the fuck you get for tryna front. Lying to kick it. I never saw you as the type," Deshawn chuckled as he sparked a blunt.

After a couple hours of anxiously waiting for Namiko to return, my phone buzzed.

***Kiyuki:*** *We're here.*

I closed my phone and ran out back with Deshawn right behind me. When I got outside, I only saw Kiyuki, but with both bags.

"Where is Namiko?" I asked as she handed us the bags.

"She handed me her bag and headed home," Kiyuki replied, and followed Deshawn back into the club.

*What the fuck man...*

# NAMIKO

I'd been making a lot of money working for that asshole Max. It'd been a long time since I had money to just blow. I took myself shopping earlier today, and I wanted to go out and show off. I took Evelyn to the mall with me, and bought her a couple things too, so we were gonna go out together.

I looked at my iPhone, and saw Evelyn had texted that she was running a little late. I decided to pour myself a glass of wine, and relax for a bit before going. Aniku was spending the night with her friend Orianna, and Kiyuki was out doing God knows what, so I was home alone.

I turned on the show Wayward Pines via Hulu, as I damn near downed the wine. Suddenly, I heard someone ring the doorbell, and I jumped because this show was kind of creepy, putting me on edge.

"Who is it?" I yelled as I walked to the door.

"Maximilian."

I stopped in my tracks and took a deep breath. I started thinking about the last two exchanges, and wondered if he was here to kill me. I quickly checked my breath, and then twisted the knob.

"Hi Ma-"

He barged into the house, and I closed the door behind him. I had on my dress for the night, but my hair was still in its dry, messy bun, and I didn't have on shoes.

"About to go put some more miles on that pussy?" he asked looking me up and down.

He had on sweats, a t-shirt, and some Nikes. His hair was freshly cut under his hat as always. His eyes were red under his hat beak, letting me know he was faded. He clenched his jaw, and looked around the room. His dark caramel complexion seemed to have a red undertone, as if his blood was hot and begging to seep through his skin.

"Why did you come here Max?" I finally asked, ignoring his insults. He didn't respond as he walked towards me. I backed up away from him, until I hit the wall. He pressed up against me and towered over me.

"How many more niggas you about to let slide up in my pussy?" he asked with his face twisted up in anger.

"Move," I whined and tried to push his rock hard body back.

He was muscular but nowhere near buff or a body builder; he was just right. He grabbed my wrist tightly, and pinned it above my head. He reached down and grabbed the other wrist to do the same.

"Answer me Nami. How many? Five? Ten? How many you let hit already?" he barked but in a low tone. My chest heaved up and down, as I breathed every piece of air like it was my last.

"Ten!" I spat and he laughed.

"I always knew you was a slut," he said.

"Let me go," I cried feeling my hot tears on my cheeks.

He started to kiss my cheeks, and then my lips. He kissed down to my neck, and then the top of my breasts.

"Marry me Nami. I don't care if it's twenty niggas you gave it up to," he whispered, as he sucked on my lips, and hugged my waist tightly.

"You wanna get married?" I asked in a breathy tone, with my eyes shut tightly.

He continued to kiss my cheeks, lips, neck, shoulders, and the exposed parts of my breasts. He reached his hand between my legs, and began to slowly and softly massage my pussy.

"I wanna marry you, babe. I love you," he whispered.

"Max..." I exhaled between kisses.

He reached under my dress, and ripped my thin lace panties. He rubbed his fingers across my soaking wet vagina, and started to ease his way to my opening.

"Max wait. I'm still a virgin," I admitted looking up into his eyes.

"I thought you said you-"

"I lied Max," I said shaking my head.

"You still wanted to marry me thinking I slept around?" I asked cupping his face.

"Unfortunately ma," he responded and pecked my lips.

The next morning, we headed to get our marriage license, and then went to get married at Elope in Michigan down in Ann Arbor. It's the same as going to the courthouse, but just a little more romantic. No one was there but Max, me of course, and Konz as a witness.

After sharing our first kiss as a married couple, we got a room at the Holiday Inn nearby because Max said he couldn't wait to consummate the marriage. There weren't any nice hotels around the area, but this was the best one. By now, it was around 7pm at night.

"I can't believe we did that," I smiled and exhaled.

"I know. Me either. How does it feel to be Namiko Davis?" he asked.

"It's the best feeling in the world," I said standing up to undress.

Max watched me closely, as I stripped down to my birthday suit. Once I was naked, he did the same and then we climbed into bed. He got between my legs, and cupped my breasts to suck on my nipples. He sucked them hard, and it sent shock waves through my body. The room was dark except for the one lit candle that we'd bought from the store. He kissed between my breasts and then down to my vagina. He spread my legs slowly and stared at it for a couple seconds.

"Is something wrong?" I asked worried.

He didn't answer as he started to flick his tongue over my pearl. He sucked on it softly, making me arch my back in pleasure. He placed his hands on my inner thighs to keep me from closing my legs, as he attacked my pussy.

"Ahhh Max! Uhhh, oh my gosh," I moaned as I came all over his soft full lips.

He licked between the slit, and then kissed it before standing on his knees. His long thick dick stood at attention, and scared was an understatement.

"You're gonna put the whole thing in?" I asked and he smirked.

He stroked it slowly, and then lowered himself between my legs. He tongued me down, as he pushed my legs back slightly.

"Don't we need protection?" I asked.

"I don't wanna use any," he replied. "Married people don't use protection," he whispered as he sucked my lips.

I felt his thick head at my small opening, and my legs started to tremble in fear. He placed his hands under my knees, and pushed my legs back some. He started to press his dick into me, and it felt like I was being ripped in half.

"Max," I whispered as tears left my eyes due to the pain. He bit his lip, as he watched his dick continue to force its way inside me.

"You feel so good already," he moaned.

He pushed, and pushed, and I prayed for him to run out of dick already. I felt him in my stomach, as he finally let a moan escape his mouth, letting me know he was finally all the way inside me.

"This is unreal right now," he said in a low tone as he pumped me slowly.

"Uhhh Ma-" I tried to say but he dropped down onto me and tongued me down.

We were kissing so hard, and his tongue was so far in my mouth, that I could barely moan. The pain was indescribable, as he sped up his pumps a little bit. With every thrust, I felt like I was splitting in half. However, there was a slight bit of pleasure to it. I caressed the back of his head, as the pain and pleasure started to become 50/50 instead of 95/5.

"Fuck. I'm about to nut," he said speeding it up.

"Slow down babe, please," I pleaded into his mouth as we kissed.

"I need you to be a big girl Nami," he whispered back as he pulverized my once virgin walls.

"Ahhhh, uhhhh," I moaned into his mouth. He leaned up off me a bit, and I placed my hand at his pelvis to slow him down.

"Get your hand out of the way," he ordered as he slowed down his strokes. I did as I was told, and he pinned my hands above my head. "As long as you have air in your lungs, this pussy belongs to me," he said sternly as he slowly pumped in a circular motion. "Fuck. Ah." He bit his lip and sped back up. He hugged me tightly, as he pounded away, and I felt myself release on him. "I want you to cum on it again for me," he said as he sucked my lips. He kept pumping at a medium pace, with my hands pinned behind my head. "Give it to me," he moaned into my mouth, and on cue I came again. "Shit. I'm right behind you," he moaned and shot off inside me. "Oh, fuck!" he yelled in a low tone.

"I love you Max," I moaned as he stared into my eyes.

He breathed heavily and then kissed my lips. He fucked me all night until it was light outside. Between my legs, it was so sore that I couldn't sit up in the bed, or lay on my sides. For the first few times I peed, there was blood when I wiped.

The next day, I could barely walk without it hurting, and during the car ride home, I had to sit on the edge of the seat in order to not press up against my sore vagina. It was all worth it though. I made love to the man I loved, while keeping my promise to my parents. As of right now, life was good.

# MAXIMILIAN

I was a married man. Wow. I admit I was in my feelings and caught up in the moment when I proposed, but I didn't regret it. I could barely sleep at night, with the thought of Namiko out in these streets spreading her legs for random niggas. I finally said fuck it and rushed to her crib, and then ended up proposing. I was happy though, because I was definitely in love with Namiko.

"You okay babe?" I smiled and looked over at her in the passenger seat. She appeared to be in a little pain, but she tried to mask it.

"You wore me out last night," she grinned, flashing her pretty ass teeth.

"That was a year of fucks I had to get out," I joked.

"You're so nasty," she chuckled.

"I can be," I nodded.

My phone started to ring, and I looked down quickly to see Cori's name flash across. I had totally forgotten that she was currently my damn girlfriend. I had yet to break up with her, and she was even next to me in the bed when I hopped up to go see Namiko.

"I'm done drop you off at your crib, aight ma?" I spoke up.

"Why Max?" she frowned.

"I got to handle some stuff," I shrugged. "We're married now though; I should be at your house," she whined.

"Look Nami, I'm taking you to your house, and I will come get you later," I spat, wanting to end this conversation.

"I knew marrying you was a mistake," she said in a low tone, and folded her arms over her small breasts.

"Well too bad. You're mine now, and you gone be forever. So get over the regret, it won't help," I replied.

I pulled up to her house and parked my whip. I got out and walked around to open the door for her. She shook her head, as a single tear slid down out of her slanted eyes, onto her dark caramel cheek.

"Come on and get out Nami," I exhaled heavily.

She got out the car and headed towards her house. I grabbed her bag out of the backseat and followed her up the walkway.

"Aye, come here," I said pulling her arm to turn her around. "Stop fucking crying Namiko. I love you, and I'm gone be back to get you in a little bit. We only been married some odd hours, and you that attached to a nigga already?" I joked trying to lighten up the mood.

"I'm not attached to you at all," she said matter-of-factly.

"Why you crying then?" I smiled. She shrugged her shoulders and I laughed. "Gimme a kiss sexy," I said biting my lip. She looked up into my eyes as I towered over her. I pressed my lips against her soft ones, and she finally unfolded her arms to place her hands on my abs.

"I love you Max," she whispered.

"I know," I smirked and jogged back to my car. She watched me for a bit, then headed inside her house.

I drove fast to my house, so I could hurry up and kick Cori out. I felt bad as hell that I was about to do her like this, but I had no choice. I was married to Namiko now, and we had to live together. On top of that, I didn't want to be with Cori anyway, so what better reason to kick her out.

"Where have you been all damn night?" Cori glared at me when I walked into the den area.

"I had some business to handle," I shrugged.

"By yourself? Cause my brother wasn't with you, and Larry was at Red Sugar all night." She raised a brow like I was scared of her ass.

"Yeah I went by my fucking self, is there a problem?" I mugged her.

"Yes! I'm your woman! You need to communicate with me when you're gonna be gone like that nigga! What if something happened to you!" she screamed.

"Look, I need to talk to you about something," I replied dryly.

"What!" she yelled, obviously still stuck in her ranting mood.

"Me and uh, Namiko got married and she's moving in so you gotta go," I said. I know I didn't lay it out in the best way possible, but I just wanted to get this over with.

"Wait, let me make sure I understand the shit that just spilled from your cheating ass lips! You left me, your woman, alone all night so you could marry another bitch? Not fuck, not get some head, but marry? I've heard of niggas having babies on bitches but not getting wives on bitches," she scoffed and paced the den. I didn't care about her theatrics; I just needed her out so I could go get my wife before she tried to file for divorce. "So where does that leave me Max?" she asked in a calmer tone; however, now tears were free falling from her eyes.

"Cori, you knew I didn't want this," was all I could say.

"But you said you would try!" she yelled.

"I did fucking try! We been together for four months, and I have yet to feel anything for you that was beyond sexual," I hollered back.

"Four months ain't shit Max! You gave that Asian hoe a fucking year almost!" she shouted with spit flying everywhere.

"That was different."

"Yeah it was, you pussy ass nigga! You out here marrying bitches just so you can hit. You're pathetic," she laughed.

"I married her because I loved her. I love Namiko. An emotion I will never feel for you," I scowled. I hated to do my best friend's sister like this, but she was pushing me. "Now get the fuck out my crib Cori. If I have to ask you again, I'm gone lay you out." I clenched my jaw because I was so angry.

"You said you would try," she started to sob uncontrollably. She knew a woman crying was my weak spot. A crying woman could make me do anything.

"Cori, stop ma," I said hugging her and rubbing her back.

"One week. I just need one week to prove to you that you made a mistake Max," she said looking up into my eyes.

Her smooth brown skin was perfection, right along with her full lips and perfect teeth. Cori was thick as fuck too, nothing like Nami. She had thick thighs, a big round ass, big titties, and thick hips. Her stomach wasn't flat, but she still looked good as hell. She could be a plus-size model for sure. Namiko wasn't skinny, but she definitely wasn't thick. It was probably the Asian in her that made her small, but the black part in her gave her a little meat on her bones. The black part gave her a small plump ass and nice size thighs.

"Please," she pleaded looking up into my eyes.

"Aight Cori, one week," I replied dumbly. *Really Max? You're married nigga!* I thought.

"Yes! I love you baby!" She smiled and hugged me tight.

I let my hands roam her thick body, and then squeezed her ass. *What was I doing? But shit, at least Namiko was my wife now, and couldn't go too far.* I smiled at the thought, and then quickly shook it from my mind.

"You still need to go back to your own crib Cori," I exhaled and backed away from her.

"Okay baby. Want to have a little fun first?" she smirked as she ran a finger down my upper body.

"Maybe later," I lied and fake smiled.

I loved Namiko, and I was not about to start our marriage off by being unfaithful; I just wasn't that type of nigga. I've told myself over the years that when I found that one, I wouldn't do anything to jeopardize it. All I needed to do now was figure out how to ease Cori out of my life romantically.

# NAMIKO DAVIS

The clock read 10pm, and Max still hadn't come by to get me. Everything felt so right when we got married twenty-four hours ago, but now it all felt so wrong. I was honestly regretting the decision to marry him.

"I can't believe you did this Namiko!" my sister Kiyuki yelled.

"I know Yuki. Just stop. We need to figure out how I can get a divorce," I said crying.

"You married this nigga after I told you he was a player, and that I had sex with him." Kiyuki shook her head as Aniku covered her mouth in shock.

"What did he say about fucking Kiyuki?" Aniku frowned and shook her head. I shrugged because I forgot about that. I was so caught up, like I always am around him, that I completely forgot he had a threesome with Kiyuki.

"You're so fucking dumb yo." Kiyuki laughed in an irritated fashion. Just then, my phone started to ring and it was Maximilian.

"This is him," I said so they would be quiet.

"Put his ass on speaker," Kiyuki spat, and I did as she asked.

"Hello," I answered.

"I'm outside baby," he said.

His voice sent chills down my back, and I wasn't even mad at him anymore. The sound of him calling me baby, made me turn from a brick wall into a bowl of porridge. Kiyuki gave me a look telling me to grill him.

"Namiko?" he asked because I hadn't answered yet.

"Wh-where were you Max?" I asked nervously.

"I'll talk to you about that when we get to the house," he replied. Kiyuki bucked her eyes at me. "Did you have sex with Kiyuki?" I finally asked after a couple seconds of silence. The line went dead, and we immediately heard loud knocking at the front door.

"Open this fucking door Nami!" Max yelled from outside. Kiyuki stormed to the living room, and snatched the door open. Before she could speak, Max stormed into the house and snatched me up. "Don't you ever put me on speaker phone for people to hear, especially trying to grill me at the same time." He glared down at me.

"Let me go Max!" I said snatching my arm from him.

"Let's go, Namiko," he replied sternly.

"She ain't going nowhere," Kiyuki spoke up.

"If you want to keep your job, you'll shut the fuck up ma," Max spat, and Kiyuki just shook her head.

Aniku stared at Max in horror, as he tugged me out of the house and into his car. "I can't believe you slept with my sister," I said as soon as he started to drive. He ignored me and turned his radio up loud.

After about thirty minutes, we pulled up to his house and went inside. He grabbed me and tongued me down, until we made it to the den. He ripped my tube dress in half, vertically, and then ripped my panties off.

"Stop Max! We need to talk!" I said mushing his head back. He exhaled and then plopped down on the couch next to me.

We hadn't been married for two days, and it felt like it was already crashing and burning. I sat up on the couch, naked as the day I was born, since my clothes were ripped and on the floor. I used my forearm to cover what little breasts I had, and then looked over at Max who was angrily staring straight ahead.

"I want a divorce," I said barely above a whisper.

"Too bad, next subject," he spat without looking at me.

"I don't want to be with you anymore," I started to cry.

"Why?" he frowned finally looking at me. He was so gorgeous, and I loved him more than I loved myself, which was never a good combination.

"Cause you don't love me. You only married me to have sex with me," I sniffled. He scooted closer to me, and although butt naked, I became warm all over in the cold room.

"I married you because I love you baby. I just had something to do today. That was it. I would've never came back for you if that's all I wanted," he said in a loving tone. Or maybe I was just so into him, that it seemed to come out loving. I couldn't tell the difference anymore. He dipped his tongue in my mouth, and moved my arm off my breasts.

"Did you sleep with my sister?" I asked as he wrestled with my tongue.

"Un uhn," he quickly replied spreading my legs. I didn't know what to say, so I stayed silent. He said no, and I had no proof. What more was there to say?

I removed his shirt, and he unbuckled his jeans as we continued to kiss. He released his monster, and dimmed the lights in the room. He put his dick head at my opening, and I tried to focus on kissing to stay relaxed.

"Uhhhhhh Max!" I cried out as he pushed into me. I was still sore from last night, and that plus the pain from him tearing me open, was out of this world. He held me tightly in his strong arms, and slowly pumped into me. "Ahhh, uhhhh!" I moaned.

"Fuck Nami," he said in a low tone as he sucked my lips. "You about to have my baby," he whispered. "Tell me you gone have my baby," he demanded.

"I'm gonna have your baby," I replied as he bit my neck.

He cupped my small breasts, and sucked my nipples hungrily. I came on his pole, and he started to kiss down my toned stomach. Once he made it between my legs, he sucked my clit until I came three times. I was spent, but he came back up and plunged back inside me.

He beat my pussy up until we both exploded. We laid there out of breath, and kissing for about thirty minutes.

"I love you Mrs. Davis," he said.

"I love you too, Mr. Davis," I replied as he started to stroke me again.

# NAMIKO

I woke up and saw that Max was no longer lying next to me in bed. I exhaled heavily and shook my head. This couldn't be all marriage consisted of. So far, all we did was have sex, talk very little, and have sex some more. I wanted to go places, and watch movies like we used to do.

I got up slowly and limped to the bathroom so I could take a shower. I felt like there was a permanent gap between my legs from all the fucking Max and I were doing. I decided to take a bath instead, since I wanted to soak my bottom half. After my hot bath, I got dressed and went down to Red Sugar. Since my husband had to work so much, I was coming to work with his ass. I smiled down at my nice big ring, as I walked out of the door.

When I got to Red Sugar, it was already 4pm, and people were starting to pile in. I couldn't believe some of these men were here this damn early. That was so damn thirsty to me. It made me realize why some women didn't want their men coming to strip clubs. I shook my head in disapproval, and then headed to the back so I could see Max. I tried to walk as normal as possible while doing so.

"You married my man bitch!" I heard someone yell as I was yanked back by my hair.

I hit the ground and Cori climbed on top of me. She crushed my stomach as she straddled me, and rained blows onto my face. I tried hitting her back a couple times but her weight on my stomach was hindering me.

"Aye, chill out!" the bouncer shouted as he grabbed Cori off me.

I could taste blood in my mouth and my eye was throbbing. I coughed a bit, as I watched Cori squirm in the bouncer's arms. I limped over to her as fast as I could, and punched her so hard her head snapped back. I thought I killed her by how hard it flew backwards.

"Back the fuck up Nami!" Larry yelled pulling me away.

"Stay away from my nigga, you stupid slut ass bitch!" Cori hollered.

"Let me go!" I screamed through tears at Larry.

He let me go, and I rushed to Max's office and burst in. I didn't care what he was doing, I was mad as hell.

"Namiko? Baby what happened?" he asked getting up from behind his desk.

"Cori! Are you still fucking her?" I yelled. He didn't say anything as he walked closer to me to touch me. "No! Stop! Are you fucking her?" I yelled again as I moved back.

"No! I'm not fucking anybody but you," he replied frustrated. "Now come here so I can look at you," he frowned. I stood in the same spot, so he walked over to me. He towered over me, and inspected my face. "You still the prettiest girl I know," he smirked and pecked my lips. "Wait here," he said and rushed out his office.

Next thing I knew, loud voices were being heard all throughout the hallway. I rushed out despite Max telling me to stay put, and witnessed him going ham on Cori. She was crying hysterically and tried to hug him, but he pushed her off.

"You promised!" she kept crying.

"Go home Cori, I will holla at you later," Max replied in a calmer tone.

"You promise?" she asked and he nodded.

I rushed back into his office, so he wouldn't know I was listening. He walked in, closed the door, and smiled at me.

"What are you doing Max?" I asked.

"What you mean babe?" he frowned.

"Why are you coddling her after what she did to my face?" I grimaced.

"I was just trying to get her out of here ma," he shrugged.

"I don't want this Max. I don't want to be with you," I said feeling tears well up.

"Why Namiko?" he yelled.

"Cause you ain't shit! I know you fucking her! I wish I could take back marrying you and giving up my virginity. I really want a divorce. Please give me one," I pleaded.

"We've only been married three days and you want out?" He frowned and walked up to me.

"I married you thinking you were someone else," I cried. I plopped down on the couch and began to cry the hardest I ever cried in my life. "I'm so unhappy Max, please let me go," I sobbed.

He blew out hot air and sat next me. He grabbed my wet face and kissed my lips gently.

"How can I make you happy baby? I don't want a divorce. I want you so bad Nami," he said in a low tone as he brought me close to him.

"I need you to love me and leave any girls you have alone Max," I cried. My body jerked in his strong arms as he hugged me tight.

"Ain't no other girls baby. But I'm gonna do better," he replied kissing my neck. I was just sniffling at this point, and no new tears were falling. "I wanna make you happy," he added. He kissed me passionately and then rubbed his hands down into my sweat shorts.

"I don't want to Max," I said stopping him.

"Why?" he asked in a low tone.

"I'm just not interested in having sex with you anymore, right now," I replied honestly. I was so mad and heartbroken; the last thing I wanted was him inside me.

"Damn," he said as if I hurt his feelings.

"Well what you wanna do? You wanna go out? Can I still take you out or you don't want that either?" he asked flashing his perfect smile.

"You can take me out," I said trying to smile.

"What about your face Nami?" he asked, as he looked it over.

"I have experience covering up this stuff," I chuckled lightly.

"You had a guy who hit you?" he quizzed and seemed to be getting upset.

"No, my father when he was alive," I replied.

"I'm sorry baby," he said as he kissed all over my face. "I love you so much Namiko. You still love your husband?" he asked.

"Yeah," I replied and my voice cracked slightly.

"Thank God," he replied and dipped his sweet tongue into my mouth.

# MAXIMILIAN

I loved my wife. Whether my actions showed it or not, I was in love and deep too. I needed to let Cori go for good, and not allow her to poke my soft spot. Her putting hands on Namiko was crossing the fucking line. She lucky I ain't the type to hit females, or I would have slapped her stupid ass all around the fucking club.

Seeing Namiko cry like that, and say how unhappy she was, broke my heart. I felt like a failure. I was only a husband for three days and my wife was already saying she wanted out, and crying about how sad I made her. If all she needed was my love and faithfulness, she would get it. I had plenty of love to give her, and I had no intentions of cheating as long as I could get rid of Cori. I had a couple other hoes from the past, but once I ignored their texts for a couple weeks, they would drop off like flies.

"Open the fucking door!" I shouted as I banged on Cori's apartment door.

"Okay! Okay!" she yelled from inside. A couple seconds later, she opened the door with a bag of freezer corn on her nose. "Your little green card wife busted my shit." Cori rolled her eyes and closed the door behind me.

"That's what the fuck you get," I spat and sat down on her couch.

"But anyway, I miss you. Even though you made me move back home," she smirked.

"Back home? I never moved you in." I frowned and shook my head.

"Yeah because-"

"Anyway! Cori, this shit is done, aight ma? I'm married and you need to move on. We don't have chemistry outside of the bedroom, and I'm tired of giving you these stupid ass trial runs," I said standing back up. I wanted to leave before the waterworks started.

"Max! This is not fucking fair! You know you only married her for some pussy!" she hollered.

"I married her 'cause I love her Cori. How many times do I have to tell your brick head ass that? I'm in love with Namiko. I would've married her regardless of her morals ma," I said, almost in a pleading tone. I needed Cori to be gone.

She stood her thick ass up, and dropped her robe to the floor. She looked good as hell. I didn't discriminate; I liked girls of all shades, shapes, and sizes. As long as the pussy was good and they could hold a conversation, I was good.

"I'm out. We over. Don't hit me," I replied and then left her crib. She wasn't about to catch me slipping. I ignored her calls after me, and sped home to get ready for my date with my wife.

"You look beautiful Nami," I smiled as she walked into the foyer.

She wore a simple red dress that hugged her small yet shapely body. Her small breasts were pushed up, and appeared to be a size bigger. Her nice round ass made my dick hard immediately. I walked up to her, and moved her long dark hair behind her ear. I stared into her big but slanted honey eyes, and just admired what was mine.

"Let's go," I finally said, after pecking her lips lightly.

We entered The Rattlesnake Club on River Place Drive, which was real upscale and pricey. I didn't mind spending racks for my woman though.

"This is really nice Max." She smiled and looked around.

"I'm sorry for how I've been treating you Namiko," I said, kissing the back of her hand. She didn't say anything and just looked away. I saw her eyes were glossy, so I knew she wanted to cry. "I still have a chance to make you happy right?" I asked and she shrugged. "I hurt you that bad baby?" I frowned in confusion.

"I'm scared," she finally said.

"Of what?" I asked.

"That you're gonna turn into someone else, and I'm gonna be stuck in this with you," she sniffled.

She really had a nigga feeling like shit right now. I exhaled because I didn't know what to say. I didn't want my first marriage to be like this. I loved Namiko and I didn't want her wishing she could go back in time. I didn't want her regretting me every time she saw my face.

"I'm gone always be the man you fell in love with," I said.

"I hope so," she replied and dabbed her eyes.

"We used to have a lot of fun together Nami, remember?" I smiled and so did she. "Nothing is gonna change baby. Except now we're able to make love," I added.

"Am I good?" she asked.

"Good?"

"Is it good, like when we... make love?" she asked.

"Come here," I said pulling her close to me. "You the best I ever had," I smirked.

"No I'm not," she chuckled.

"Yes you are. I can go into detail, but I'm sure you don't want that." I smiled and she laughed. "I love your smile baby. I want to always put that on your face," I said.

She just stared into my eyes, so I pressed my lips against hers. I didn't care about the deep red lipstick she had on.

"I love you Max," she whispered, as I sucked her lips.

"I love you more. Especially that wet, tight, warm, voodoo you got between your legs," I added and she gasped.

"That's nasty," she turned her lip up.

"Even better when you cum on it, and the faces you make. Oh my God," I added and even started to get flashbacks.

"Stop!" she chuckled.

"Do you think you'll be interested any time soon?" I asked hoping she said yes. My dick was begging to be inside her again. She shrugged her shoulders and looked away. "Look at me. That's not why I married you. I spent a year with you without hitting, so I'm sure I can handle this little time out you putting me on," I grinned.

"You bet not have sex with anyone else." She raised a brow.

"No one," I assured her and she smiled. I pecked her back to back a couple times, and then we proceeded to eat dinner.

Afterwards, we went to some little lounge club, to relax and listen to some of the poetry and live acts.

"I missed hanging out with you," Namiko said as we walked into our home.

"See, I told you we could still have fun together," I replied hugging her from behind.

I kissed on her neck and shoulders as we walked up the stairs together. We undressed down to our sleepwear, and then cuddled in bed together. It was easier to hold off on sex before, but I think now that I know how good she feels, it was gonna be harder. It was like she had crack between her legs. I would lie, rob, and kill for that pussy.

We were watching a movie and the lights were out. The TV lit up the room just enough to where I could see the side of her small breast, and her hard nipples poking through the gown. The TV illuminated her dark caramel skin, and it prompted me to kiss her soft cheek. I went from her cheek, to her lips, and then tongued her down. I made my way between her legs, and then wrapped them around my waist.

"Max, I really don't want to," she whispered.

"Just let me taste you. That's it." She looked away as if she was thinking. While she was pondering, I was removing her thin lace thong.

"Only for a little bit," she replied and smirked.

Before she could finish, my head was between her legs, sucking up her sweet nectar. She tasted so sweet to me, and I loved it. Only for a little bit my ass. About twenty minutes and four orgasms later, she was begging me to stop.

"Maxxxx... I can't cum anymore." She moaned a couple seconds before releasing into my mouth a fifth time.

I looked up at her face, and a tear was rolling down her cheek. Damn I was good. I licked her clean, and then planted a kiss on her soft slit. I smiled and then went up to kiss her perfect, full lips.

"I told you only for a little bit," she smirked and I chuckled. I felt her legs trembling a little, as I kissed and kissed her.

# KIYUKI

Namiko was so damn dumb. Max was a dog and there was nothing else to it. Yeah I wanted him for myself, but I could handle a nigga like him. You think he would've left me at home until ten at night? No the fuck he wouldn't have. I really did my best to keep her away from him, but she acted like she just couldn't leave him alone. However, while working on getting my man, I had plans to put strain on their little marriage. You see, Max was all about his fucking money, and what better way to fuck with him.

"Haven't seen you in forever." I smiled at Namiko as I entered Max's office. She'd moved in with Max so she was never 'home' with Aniku and I.

Aniku told me that Namiko was holding out on Max, so I knew he'd be interested in any pussy thrown his way at this point. He'd better prepare himself, because this one was coming his way soon... again.

"I know." Namiko smiled and then looked at her 'husband'. He stared her down lustfully, and she blushed; full-fist gag.

"Y'all know what to do," Max said handing over the folders.

He then pulled Namiko close, and kissed her passionately; maybe he did love her too. Doesn't matter, I had my eyes set on him first.

"Can't wait to get this over with," Namiko exhaled when we got into the car.

"Why, so you can go home and not have a life outside of Max?" I spat.

"I do have a life outside of Max. I go to school," she replied.

"I go to school," I mocked her in a baby voice. "School ain't shit. Having a life means going out and on dates and shit. Spending niggas' money even though you got your own. That's having a life." I turned my lip up at her stupidity.

"I'm married; I can't go on dates Kiyuki. Come on now. Plus, Max takes me on plenty of dates," she replied shaking her head.

"Yeah, *you're* married, but is Max?" I asked and cracked up laughing.

"What?" she frowned.

"I got to sample that again. I did it for you though. To show you he will never change Nami. All he wanted was your virginity."

I looked over at her, and saw a tear roll down her cheek as she stared out her window. *Good job Kiyuki,* I told myself. I loved Namiko and she needed to be with a square, not a boss like Max.

"The gas light is on Yuki; you didn't get gas before we left?" Nami frowned and sniffled. I half smiled because my plan was about to take effect.

"Shit. I forgot. Max is gonna kill me if we're late because I pulled over," I replied.

"I will talk to him," she nodded.

I spotted the gas station that I had planned to stop at, and pulled over. I got out to go inside, and pay with the card Max had given us for gas, hotels, and food just in case. I went behind one of the aisles, and watched intently as my homeboy, Jared, creeped up to the SUV. I watched as he robbed Namiko at gunpoint for the drugs. It was night-time, and the gas attendant was too busy flipping through a magazine to even see what was going on outside. I parked at the furthest pump anyway. *He better not hurt her,* I said to myself. I gave Jared strict instructions, which said to take the drugs and not to hurt Namiko. I wanted to hurt her internally, not physically. I paid the attendant, and then headed outside. Jared saw me and knew it was his cue to run off.

"Kiyuki! He took the bag!" Namiko yelled.

"Namiko, shut up! You want everyone knowing what we do?" I said through gritted teeth.

No one was out there but us, but you never know who's hiding out. She folded her arms over her chest and frowned.

"We just have to head back and let Max know what happened," I shrugged.

"What are we gonna tell him?" she asked.

"We? No you, if he thinks I was included he'd kill me Nami. You're his wife, he will let this slide," I said with pleading eyes.

"Okay Kiyuki." She sighed and got back in the car.

After pumping gas, we turned around to head back to Red Sugar. It was hard as hell to keep from smiling or bursting into laughter. We took a couple deep breaths, and headed into the building and into Max's office.

"Why y'all ain't tell us you were here?" Deshawn asked.

"And where are the bags?" Max frowned standing up.

"M-Max, someone robbed me," Namiko stuttered.

"Robbed you? How the fuck you get robbed if you went straight to the destination? Did the client rob you?" Max bucked his eyes. Damn he was so sexy when he was mad.

"No, we- we didn't even make it there," Namiko replied nervously.

"Did someone even let the client know the time would change?" Deshawn quizzed.

"No we-"

"How and where did you get robbed?" Max cut in.

"I told Kiyuki to stop for gas and- and when I was waiting, a guy held me at gun point to get the drugs," Namiko said as she fidgeted with her fingers.

"Did they specifically ask for the drugs Nami?" Max asked as Deshawn ran a hand over his face. Fuck, I hope Jared wasn't dumb enough to ask for the drugs specifically.

"Yeah," she replied and I wanted to run out and beat Jared's ass.

"Aight, so this was an inside job. Come here baby girl. You okay?" Max questioned as he took Namiko's hand in his.

"Are you gonna kill me?" Namiko asked, and as irritated as I was by her, that shit was funny as fuck. Everyone burst into laughter, as she stared at Max with a serious expression.

"You're my wife ma. You're more important than all this shit; I wouldn't kill you over that. Only if you gave away that gold between your legs," Max answered, biting his lip.

I had to erase what he just said out of my mind, so I could enjoy the sight of him biting that sexy bottom lip. Namiko smiled and draped her arms over his shoulders.

"And on that note..." Deshawn chuckled and left, once Max and Namiko started pecking each other.

"Hold up D. We need to get together and discuss who this could've been," Max called after him. My mouth dried up, and I swallowed the lump in my throat. I prayed no one found it was me and Jared, because I was sure I'd be a goner.

❧

*BOOM! BOOM! BOOM!*

"Aye, why you beating on my door like you the po-po's?" Jared answered the door.

"Nigga, why the fuck did you specifically ask for the drugs? Now they know it was an inside job dummy!" I yelled, smacking him upside the head.

"Fuck Max. I might do that shit again since I know y'all route now," Jared smirked.

"Nigga, you better not. This was a one-time thing." I rolled my eyes.

"Was me stroking them walls a one-time thing?" he asked. I licked my lips at him as he eyed my body. Jared had at least twelve inches of dick.

"No it wasn't a one time," I replied seductively and then followed him to the bedroom.

"Ooohhh fuck!" I yelled out as Jared pumped into my walls.

He was so big, but so damn good. I was surprised Larry hadn't figured out I was fucking somebody else. Yeah, Larry and I were dating now. It was only because I wanted his money though, and I felt I needed to thank him for hooking Namiko and I up with Max.

"Shit. I'm 'bout to bust shorty," Jared moaned.

"Ahhhh. Uhhh!" we screamed out in unison, as we both came.

"You need to start strapping up nigga," I smirked.

"Maybe I want you to have my baby," he said licking his sexy lips.

"Only baby I'm pushing out is Maximilian's." I rolled my eyes and laid down next him.

"You a grimy ass hoe," he chuckled, and lit an already rolled blunt.

"Maybe I am, but I told her I wanted him and she still went after him, so who is really the hoe?" I raised a brow.

"I guess she shady too." He shrugged and took a pull before passing it.

"Has he even hit yet?" Jared asked with a raised brow.

"Wouldn't you like to know," I laughed and blew out smoke.

# NAMIKO

I was laying here staring up at the ceiling, as Max kissed on my neck, while rubbing his hands up my nightshirt. All I could think about was the fact that Kiyuki said she slept with him- again.

As he pulled my panties down, ready to end the drought we'd been on, I stopped him. "Nami, come on ma. I'm dying here," he groaned as he stood up on his knees.

"Did you fuck my sister again?" I asked ignoring his complaints.

"Why do you keep asking me that? Who is telling you that I slept with your sister?" he frowned.

"Doesn't matter Max. Did you or not?" I repeated my question.

"No Namiko. I've never touched your sister." He shook his head and then laid next me. He exhaled heavily and then turned his back to me.

"What are you doing?" I frowned.

"I'm going to sleep," he spat.

"Why?"

"I'm not in the mood anymore ma," he replied dryly.

Regardless of how much we loved one another, I knew sex was a big part of a relationship. I didn't want to lose my man over something so small. I wanted to have sex with him, I just held back until I felt like he deserved it and was being true to me.

I tugged on his shoulder, and he slowly laid on his back. I removed my nightshirt and straddled his waist slowly. He ran his strong hands all over my naked body, as he bit his lip. I loved the feeling of his hands on me; I missed making love just as much as him. He squeezed my breasts gently, as I pushed his boxers down. I positioned myself above his dick and slowly slid down on it. I tried to hide the pain I was feeling, so that I could perform successfully.

"Damn. Just like that Nami," Max panted.

"Uuhhhh. Ahhhh," I cried out as I felt my orgasm rising already. Max grabbed and smacked my ass, as I rocked my hips, bouncing up and down.

He ran his hands up and down my back, and I shivered at his touch. I looked down as his sexy face, as he watched me ride his dick. He let out a couple soft moans and bit his lip, as he stared me in the eyes. My man was the finest nigga in Detroit.

"Bounce on it Namiko," he ordered, and I did just that.

The sound of him going in and out of me was like a beautiful symphony and I came immediately. He covered my small breasts with his big strong hands, and squeezed them around the sides. He sat up, and sucked my nipples like he wanted to get the gold out of them.

"Ooohh baby," I purred as he licked between my breasts.

He laid back down and watched his dick become covered in my juices once again. We intertwined our fingers, as I continued to bounce and rock slowly on his long thick dick. It seemed as if sparks were flying all around the room as we made love. We were connecting again, and I felt it in every stroke; we were becoming one.

"This pussy been missing me," he panted referring to me cumming again. "I'm cumming Nami. Fuck ma!" he grunted.

"Me too daddy. Damn," I whimpered, as I made all kinds of faces.

"I love your cum faces," he exhaled.

Max pulled me close to him, and dipped his tongue in my mouth as he humped upwards. The sound of our lovemaking was music to my ears, and soon enough we exploded together. I cupped his face, and we tongued each other down as we tried to catch our breath.

"We needed that Namiko," he whispered, as his hands rubbed my sweaty back.

"I know," I replied.

"Are you happier now?" he asked looking into my eyes.

"Yeah," I responded in a low tone.

I had to agree with Max. Us making love seemed to complete our relationship. Whenever we didn't, it felt like something was missing. For the first time in a long time, I was happy to be married to him.

The next day, we spent a lot of time together. We went on a boat ride, dinner, and then the movies. Maximilian was really my best friend, and I was starting to remember how much I loved being around him.

Today I needed to go talk to Kiyuki about she and Max. I didn't know whom to believe at this point. She kept saying she slept with him, and as you know, he denied it. Kiyuki has always had my back, so I couldn't imagine her lying to me.

"Hey, you busy?" I asked knocking on Kiyuki's cracked open door.

"Do I look busy?" she spat.

"I wanted to talk to you," I said as I walked in and sat at her desk.

"So talk," she replied as she scrolled on her iPhone.

"Max said he never slept with you," I started. "I asked him twice and he said no both times," I added.

"Of course he's gone tell you that. I bet you believe it too," she said refusing to look at me.

"I don't know what-"

"I'm your fuckin' sister Namiko! You've only known this nigga a little over a year and he already got something over me? You get shadier as time goes on." She shook her head and rolled her eyes.

"Do you have some type of proof Yuki? I mean I can't just-"

"Get the fuck out! You wanna choose that nigga over me? Get the fuck out!" she yelled and hopped up off her bed. She pulled on my arm roughly, and damn near dragged me to the door. "Bye bitch," she added and pushed me into the hallway wall.

She slammed her door and I heard her lock it. I swear she acted so fucking ridiculous sometimes. If she wasn't my sister, I would've been beat her ass.

*KNOCK! KNOCK!*

"Kiyuki! Open the door! I just want something to prove to me that he fucked you! If anyone should be mad, it should be me! He's my husband!" I shouted making her snatch the door open.

"Are you crazy? He's your husband but I told you I wanted him! You just couldn't let me be happy. You jealous as fuck, but it's cool Nami, you're gonna get yours." She smirked and folded her arms across her chest.

I walked close to her face; so close, our noses almost touched.

"Since you ain't got no proof, I'm gone assume you lying. However, you have one more time to claim you fucked my man. The next time, I'm whooping your ass Yuki." I stared into her eyes for a couple seconds, before turning around to leave.

"Nami wait," she called after me. "I'll get your proof. Just don't be mad at me okay?" she smiled sympathetically.

"Okay," I replied still angry.

I felt bad for threatening her, but I was just furious as hell. I didn't know what the fuck was going on between Kiyuki and Max, but I didn't like it. I just couldn't see my sister lying to me. Also, I couldn't see Max sleeping with her. He loved me too much, and he knows something like that would break me in two.

# MAXIMILIAN

„Y ou wanted to see me?" Kiyuki asked swinging her front
door open and grinning.

"Yeah, sit down," I ordered as I barged into her house
and sat down. I intertwined my fingers under my chin, and squinted
my eyes before speaking. "Why is Namiko asking me if I slept with
you?" I questioned getting straight to the point.

"Really?" she chuckled. "I have no idea. Maybe she just sees that we
have chemistry," she added and shrugged.

"But we don't, so that's not it. I bet not find out you feeding her
lies," I replied.

"Why would I tell my sister I slept with her husband? Does that
make sense? What would I possibly be trying to accomplish by telling
her that?" She frowned in disgust and rolled her eyes.

"I could care less about the motive. Like I said, I bet not find out
you doing anything sneaky Kiyuki."

"Or what?" she smirked.

"Or none of us will ever see you again," I responded, staring
directly into her eyes to let her know I was serious.

"Relax. Ain't nobody telling her shit. But what's up with you?

You're my brother-in-law and I feel like I don't know you," she smiled seductively.

Kiyuki, after Namiko, was hands down one of the sexiest chicks in Michigan. She was a skeezer though, and it took away from her looks.

"What you wanna know?" I asked as I checked the notifications on my iPhone.

"I don't know. Before my sister who were you with?" she raised a brow.

"I wasn't with nobody, I was dibbling and dabbling," I chuckled to myself.

"You don't see yourself ever trying out another bitch... Ever?" she quizzed and licked her lips.

Why did she have to say it like that? I could be faithful. These bitches weren't worth shit after you busted, and I wasn't about to lose my wife over they ass. But damn, when she said *ever* like that, I got a sharp pain in my body.

"Nah, I see myself only fucking with your sister, that's why we're married." I nodded to assure her.

"Damn, it's crazy because I told her I liked you before y'all even met." She smiled like she was reminiscing.

"Oh yeah?" I raised a brow.

"Yeah, I was all into you but I guess she won. All I thought about was riding and sucking your dick until you fell asleep." *Damn,* I thought. "Nami do that for you?" she inquired.

"Let's talk about something else ma." I cleared my throat.

"Why Max?" she asked standing up.

She had on a skintight bodysuit, for what reason I didn't know. Her body was super curvy, but still slim. Her and Namiko were about the same size, but she was thicker and had more breasts and ass. She was also lighter than Nami.

"Cause we shouldn't be talking about us being intimate, when I'm married to your sister," I said looking up at her pretty face.

"Well why don't we stop talking about it, and just umm, do it?" She chuckled and slowly unzipped the front of her bodysuit.

I couldn't do this shit. Not only was she my wife's sister, but I'd already led Cori on not even twenty-four hours after my wedding. I was not gone be that philandering ass, lying ass, scheming ass husband. Especially not to Namiko, she deserved better than that.

"Yo, chill out," I said putting my hand up to stop her from nearing me. She paused and turned her lip up in irritation.

"Ain't nobody gone tell Namiko nigga, damn," she damn near yelled.

"It ain't about her finding out. I don't want to do it. I only came here to talk to you and make sure you weren't in her ear with no bull-shit," I spat.

"You gone regret this Max. I'm the type of bitch you need by your side. You ain't good enough for Namiko. She needs to marry a scientist or somebody. You my type of nigga not hers!" she hollered, while pointing her finger.

"Well looks like she doesn't agree 'cause she's married to me," I said standing up. "Don't you ever push up on me again Kiyuki. As much as you think you're my type, you're not. You a sneaky ass hoe. You the type of bitch I bend over a desk, fuck, nut on her face, and never call again," I said through gritted teeth as I towered over her.

She stared up at me in disbelief. I didn't give a fuck because it was true. I would never wife a bitch like her. It amazed me that she and Namiko were even blood, but I guess it was like Konz and I.

"You can leave now," she said in a low tone, but I was already walking to the door.

"Don't be late for work tomorrow night," I said before slamming the front door.

⚜

"Man, that bitch Kiyuki is a snake dawg," I said to Deshawn as I passed him the blunt.

"She bad though," Konz chuckled.

"Nigga, that's all you think about!" Deshawn shook his head and took a pull.

"I wonder if Larry would let me bang her out one time," Konz added as he stared out the window.

"Larry fucking her?" I asked.

"Hell yeah nigga! Why you think he brought in she and Namiko for the job?" Konz frowned.

"Makes sense," I shrugged. "But Kiyuki tried to give me some pussy earlier," I said shaking my head.

"How was it?" Konz asked like a little kid wanting to hear about a new big roller coaster.

"I denied that shit. I told you I almost slipped up with Cori the day after my damn wedding. She got to crying and shit, and I almost ended up giving her thick ass some sympathy dick." I exhaled as the event replayed in my mind. "Thank God I stayed strong, but I'm on the straight and narrow my nigga."

"Nigga can we not talk about you almost dicking down my damn sister." Deshawn frowned and blew out smoke.

"Aye, yo' sister thick as fuck though. She reminds me of Toccara from that model show," Konz joked and I laughed.

"I know that pussy is good as fuck. Anytime a bitch got a little fat around her stomach, she harboring good pussy under it," Konz added, and we both started dying laughing.

"You right about that homie," I chuckled. "Namiko's stomach is flat as hell though, and her pussy just as good – maybe even better," I added.

"Only cause it's new. Wait until that pussy get a few miles on it," Konz replied.

"It ain't gone get no miles on it unless I'm the one putting them on there," I snapped back.

"Man that's now. Once y'all been married for a while, she gone get tired of that same old dick and you gone get tired of that same old pussy. Y'all gone be fucking other people so much, people gone think it's an open marriage." Konz laughed and so did Deshawn.

"And any nigga that slide his dick in my bitch getting a bullet to the dome," I spat and fake laughed. This nigga had the game fucked up and twisted up if he thought I was gone let a nigga smash Namiko and live to tell about it.

"Ah fuck. Chill out big bro'. I'm just fucking with you. I know you sensitive about lil' Nantucket," he laughed and took a pull.

"Man, fuck you!" I laughed.

"You still mad about us talking about Cori?" I joked with Deshawn cause that nigga was quiet.

"I told y'all about that bullshit," he scoffed.

"You should be proud yo' sister got some good pussy!" I joked and Konz and I died laughing.

Deshawn tried to a keep a straight face, but a smile was tugging at the corner of his mouth. "I hate y'all niggas," he finally chuckled.

# NAMIKO

Maximilian and I had been perfect so far. Married life was everything that I dreamed of, despite our beyond rocky start. We had yet to have our honeymoon, so we were gonna go to Las Vegas, Nevada to celebrate. Max suggested somewhere more romantic like France or Italy, but Vegas seemed more exciting.

"So you gonna come?" I asked my best friend Evelyn.

"What does his homeboy look like?" she asked turning her lip up.

"Hold on," I said pulling out my phone to go on his Instagram.

"This is him. His name is Deshawn." I smiled and showed her my phone.

"Oh hell nah bitch, this nigga ugly as fuck!" she yelled, and started scrolling through more of his pictures.

Deshawn was an okay looking guy to me. He was light skinned, had a goatee, low cut curly fade, and dressed nice. He was no Maximilian, but he was cool. He was more so a pretty boy than anything.

"Well then can you just come? Deshawn is coming and I promised him I had a friend," I smiled at her crazy ass.

"You know I don't like them light-brights. I'm light enough," she pouted.

Evelyn had a smooth toasted vanilla complexion, pouty lips, thick ass frame, and a short curly fro. She was beautiful, and only liked brown to dark skinned guys. She said she didn't like them light, because she didn't want clear kids.

"Pleeeaaassseeeeee!" I fake pouted and put my hands up in mock prayer.

"I guess," she replied, sucking her teeth and rolling her eyes. "But I ain't paying for shit!" she said, pointing one of her freshly manicured nails in my face.

"Max and Deshawn are footing the bill." I shook my head at her. "Okay, let's go to the grocery store. I need to make dinner for my huuuusssbbbaaannnnd," I said swaying my body.

"You are so annoying." Evelyn laughed and lightly pushed me towards the door. "You need to be finding me one, instead of shaking your little ass," she added as we headed to the car.

After getting everything I needed, we headed out to the parking lot. When I neared my car, I realized my tires were on four flats. My all-white 2005 Toyota Corolla looked a mess. With my mouth ajar, I walked over to the side of my car, and saw 'Man Stealing Bitch' spray painted in red.

"Who the fuck did this?" Evelyn asked as she looked on in shock.

"I'm pretty sure it was Cori's stupid ass," I exhaled.

"Let's just load this stuff up," I said shaking my head.

I had my car towed to my house, since it had the groceries in it, and then called Max to see where he was.

"Hello?" he answered.

"Your little side hoe fucked my car up," I said through gritted teeth.

"Who?" I could tell he was frowning.

"Cori! She slashed my tires and spray painted my car!" I yelled.

"Calm the fuck down Namiko! Now how do you know it was her?" he inquired.

"Who the fuck else? How many hoes do you have!" I screamed into the phone.

"I told you to calm the fuck down. I didn't mess your car up. I'm on my way home," he spat then hung up.

"What he say?" Evelyn asked as she finished putting up the groceries.

"He's on his way," I replied as I plopped down on the barstool.

"Well that's my cue. I'm not tryna see y'all fuss and fuck," she joked and we chuckled.

"Okay bye." I half smiled.

I left the kitchen and headed to the bedroom. I changed into something sexy so that Max wouldn't stay mad at me. He hated when I yelled at him. *"Don't talk to me like a child Namiko. I'm your man."* I got turned on as I thought about when he said that to me.

After about ten minutes of being fully dressed in my blue lace thong and bra set, I heard him coming up the stairs.

"You think you slick." He smiled when he saw me. He strolled over to me and started to kiss my neck.

"I'm still mad about my car Max," I whined.

"I'll get you another one," he responded, brushing me off. "I've been trying to buy your stubborn ass a new car."

"What are you gonna do about her?" I quizzed.

"Who?" he asked like an idiot.

"Cori!" I pushed him off lightly.

"I'll take care of it," he responded between kisses on my small round breasts. "Now, I got something for that mouth since you can't close it," he added, as he stood up and released his beautiful caramel dick.

I started to tease the head, as he removed his shirt to expose his perfectly chiseled abs. I slowly but surely took all his ten inches into my mouth, letting my saliva coat it completely.

"Shit," he whispered.

He ran his fingers through my long dark hair, and massaged my scalp. He started to slowly hump my face, as I played with his balls.

"I'm about to cum Nami. Fuck," he grunted.

I kept up my pace, and he released his seeds down my throat in no time. He slowly slid out of my mouth, and then flipped me on all fours. He tugged my thin thong down with his teeth. I loved when he did that. I looked over my shoulder at him, as he spread my legs. He licked between my folds and my ass, making my body shiver and teeth chatter. He dropped down and tugged my clit into his mouth. He sucked it hard, while dipping his finger into my hole.

"Maxxxx, shit," I cried.

"Tastes good Nami," he moaned between licks and sucks.

He held my ass cheeks open so that he could lick and suck everywhere with unlimited access. It was so hard to keep my body from collapsing, as he sucked everything out of my body.

"Put your face into the pillow," he ordered.

I did as he asked, and boy did he really go to work. He was sucking my clit with all his neck muscles, and plunging his finger into my hole nice and slow. He was taking me over the edge, as I bit into the pillow.

"Oh my goossshhh Max!" I cried; literally a tear came out my eye.

I clutched the sheets as he ate my pussy like it was his last meal. I didn't care about anything in the world right now, other than his fierce head game.

"I'm cumming daddy. Ahhh," I whimpered and released on his full lips.

He licked me clean like a kitten, and then eased his monster into my sopping wet walls. He grabbed a handful of my hair, then rammed into me and pulled out slowly. He continuously did so, until I felt my juices running down my thighs.

"I fucking love this pussy," he said in a low tone. "It loves me too. Look how it's cumming for me back to back," he added, continuing to talk shit.

Once I came for the third time, he put me on my back and removed my bra. He devoured my nipples, while massaging my clit. I was soaking wet, and he was taking me over the edge yet again. He picked his head up and dipped his tongue into my mouth, while sliding back inside me.

"You so fucking wet," he whispered to me, while pumping me in a circular motion. He pinned my hands above my head, while continuing to tongue me down and thrust me. "Tell me you love me Nami," he panted.

"I love- ahhhh, I love you so much Max," I purred.

"Who's daddy?" he asked biting his sexy lip.

"You... daddy." I tried to smile but it quickly turned into a sex face as I came again.

"Ahhhh fuck!" he grunted as he burst inside me. "Oh, that was the shit." He exhaled heavily and sucked my lips.

I draped my arms over his shoulders and dipped my tongue into his mouth.

# NAMIKO

As we rode in the taxi to our hotel in Vegas, I admired the beautiful city. We arrived around 8pm, so it was dark outside with beautiful lights everywhere. It almost seemed like every building had decorated for the Christmas season. Just looking at it all made me feel warm inside. On top of that, everyone that lived in Vegas seemed to be out and about. I'd never seen so many people on one sidewalk. They were all walking and sight seeing; some dressed up, and some just casual. I couldn't wait to get out in the morning and visit the little shops they had along the strip, especially the fashion mall.

We finally pulled up to our hotel at the Palazzo, which appeared to be dipped in gold, and was tall as hell. I wondered if part of it was just for show, or if they really had rooms all the way up to the top. We were dead smack in the middle of the strip, just like I told Max I wanted to be.

"So, Namiko and I are in the same room right?" Evelyn chuckled as we pulled into the hotels little roundabout driveway.

"Yeah right," Max scoffed and we laughed.

Turns out Max and I were together, obviously, and Evelyn and Deshawn had their own shit separately.

"What are we doing tonight?" I asked as I laid down on the bed. Truthfully, I was tired, but I didn't want to be a party pooper.

"Well, you damn party animal, I was thinking we could just relax here in our suite for the night. We should spend some more time together," Max smiled. I loved his beautiful smile, and how his dark caramel complexion lit up when he did it.

"Okay, I'd like that. You know I love spending time with you." I smiled and stood up to walk over to him.

He was sitting on the chair in the room, so I stood in between his legs. I took off his hat so I could run my fingers through the curls of his fade. I loved doing that for some reason.

"Stop always trying to get in my pants girl," he joked and bit his lip. I loved when he bit his lip.

"Well, you're just so sexy," I smirked and straddled him.

We started to kiss one another, and my body became extremely hot. *When did I become such a sexual person?* I wondered. I started to grind my hips on him, as he rubbed his hands all over my thighs.

"You gaining a little weight baby." He looked over my body lustfully.

"I am?" I yelped.

"It's a good thing though, you look good." He smiled at my frantic reaction.

"I didn't think I was fat," I said, as I got off his lap.

"You're not fat babe. You're just a little thicker in some areas. You got a little more thighs, and ass," he replied, licking his lips and walking towards me.

"You sure?" I asked worried.

"Positive. Take your clothes off sexy," he ordered, and folded his arms across his chiseled pecks.

Before I could get my clothes off good, he rushed me onto the bed and started kissing my still flat stomach, and then my thicker thighs.

"Just stay like that for a while," he said.

"What? It's cold Max!" I laughed.

"I know, look how hard your nipples are. But just let me admire you for a little bit," he responded with a serious expression, as his eyes trailed the full length of my body. "You told me your dad used to hit you, what happened to him?" he asked. *How did we get here?* I thought.

"What?" I asked in order to stall on giving him the answer.

"Did I stutter?" He pursed his lips.

"Yeah..." I snickered.

"Then you heard me twice. Now tell me," he demanded, as he ran a single finger from my stomach to my vagina.

"He died," I exhaled.

"Oh damn, I'm sorry babe. Can I know how?" he questioned.

"I don't want to talk about it right now," I half lied. I wouldn't have minded telling him if my dad had died some other way.

*Would I ever tell him? He's my husband he should know everything about me. Maybe later,* I thought.

"Did I upset you?" he asked as he looked into my eyes.

"No," I half smiled. "What happened to your dad?" I added.

"He umm..."

"It's okay, you don't have to say it," I cut in.

"Nah babe, we're married so I want you to know everything about me," he replied, looking into my eyes. Why did he have to say that? Now I have to tell him about mine. "He was over his best friend's house one night, and when his best friend's wife came home, they got into an argument. The argument got heated, and my dad's best friend started to hit his wife. My dad, being the type of nigga he was, attempted to break it up. They got into it because my dad was scolding him for hitting his wife, and he pulled a gun out and shot my father between the eyes. The wife came and told us everything that same night," he said, staring at the wall.

A tear slid down his face, but he wiped it as soon as it fell. I sat up, and wrapped my arms around his neck. We hugged each other tight, and I closed my eyes to savor the moment. I pulled back a little so I could look into his face.

"I'm sorry Max," I finally said and kissed his lips. Our kissing became hot and heavy, but I knew I needed to tell him about my father. "I want to tell you what happened to my dad," I said, breaking our kiss.

"Okay," he panted.

"He didn't start hitting us until my mother passed, and he and alcohol became good friends. He let us know that we would have to act as wives to him, now that my mother was gone. I was scared as hell so I kept a knife under my pillow. When he came in and got on top of me, I accidentally stabbed him in the throat. I didn't mean to do that Max, I only meant to stab his shoulder but I panicked!" I pleaded as if Max were the judge deciding my fate.

"Damn babe, I'm sorry you went through that." He shook his head and caressed my face.

"You don't think I'm crazy?" I frowned in confusion.

"No," he frowned back as if I were tripping.

"But I killed my own daddy!" I damn near yelled.

"Uh, lower your voice ma," he chuckled. "Plus, if your dad wouldn't have been trying to rape his own daughter, he wouldn't be dead. That's not your fault, you were just protecting yourself," he added. He was right.

*Why should I feel guilty when he shouldn't have been trying to rape me anyway?* I thought.

"I think you're crazy for other reasons, but not that," he joked, and I pouted playfully before he pecked my lips.

"You're the first person I've ever told that to," I said. Evelyn didn't even know, and I told her everything.

"I don't mind that," he smiled, and started to kiss me passionately and slowly.

He positioned himself on top of me and we proceeded to make love -honest love.

# KIYUKI

Cori had nothing to do with slashing Namiko's tires. Yep, that was all my doing. I knew she would blame it on Cori, and that's exactly what happened. I was coming for my sister's marriage from every angle that I possibly could. I knew Namiko would become frustrated with Cori, and Cori would deny everything. Then, Nami would be mad at Max and Max would come for Cori, causing just a big ass mess. I laughed at the thought. All the while, I would be sitting back eating popcorn and enjoying the show. I would then become a friend to Max. I would be a shoulder to lean on, and then a pussy to slide in.

Namiko and our baby sister, Aniku, had gone out to the mall today, and I followed them there. I knew Max bought Namiko a new car, but she insisted on getting her old Camry fixed. I watched as she parked in the parking lot, and waited for them to exit the car. Once I saw they were far away, I grabbed the brick I'd found, and attached a little note to it. I wrote *stay away from my man or else*, in red ink, then taped it to the brick. I slowly crept up to the back of her car, and threw the brick through her back windshield. The whole damn thing shattered, and I couldn't help but giggle. I didn't expect that, but it made it even better. I quickly booked it back to my car, and sped to "my nigga's" house.

"Where the hell have you been all day?" Larry frowned.

"I've been taking care of shit. Stop tripping." I rolled my eyes and turned up my lip.

He was irritating the fuck out of me. He was always breathing down my neck, wanting to know my whereabouts, twenty-four fucking seven.

"You better not be chasing after Max still," he spat.

"Ain't nobody chasing after Max! Your crazy ass is paranoid," I said taking a pre-rolled blunt off of his coffee table.

"Yeah, you better not be. You know who that pussy belong to." He bit his lip and rubbed his hand up my thigh.

I was not in the mood to fuck with him, but I needed him as a cover in case Max thought I was sniffing behind him still.

"You know Max told me you tried to push up on him," he added, snapping me from my thoughts.

"That nigga lying," I spat.

"Is he? 'Cause all you seem to want to talk about is him and your fucking sister!" he glared.

I didn't respond as I straddled his lap. I pulled off my t-shirt, and since I had no bra on, my titties were right there in his face. As he devoured my nipples, I tried to keep myself from throwing up. Larry wasn't cute at all. He was semi-fat, brown skinned, had braids, and always dressed like the bottom feeder ass nigga that he was. After getting his fix on my nipples, he reached under my skirt and pulled my panties to the side.

"Strap up," I said placing my hand on his ashy chunky one.

He smacked his lips, and then reached into the end table drawer to retrieve a rubber. After sliding it on his okay sized dick, I slid down on it. Larry may have been fat and ugly, but he could work that mediocre dick of his.

"Fuck," he grunted under his breath.

"Damn daddy." I whispered as I closed my eyes to fantasize about Max.

Suddenly, a good visual of he and I fucking came to my mind, and I went to work on Larry. I kept my eyes shut tightly, as I bounced up and down on his dick like a champion jockey.

"Damn girl, shit," Larry moaned as he held tightly onto my perfect waist.

I dug my long nails into his shoulders as I continued to do my best. I rocked my hips as I bounced, taking both Larry and I to new heights.

"Oh fuck Max, shit!" I cried out as I felt myself about to cum.

"Bitch, what?" Larry yelled and pushed me off his dick.

"Why you do that?" I yelled back.

"You just called me Max! Get yo' hoe ass out my shit!" He glared down at me as he put his dick up.

"Fine. Fuck you," I shrugged, and grabbed my shirt off the floor.

"You won't be working for Max no more," he said, as I approached his front door to leave.

"Nigga what? Don't fuck with my money aight?" I spat and rolled my neck.

"Yeah, get the fuck out!" he screamed and gestured for me to do so.

I quickly left out his crib, happy that I would no longer have to put on a show. However, I was scared that I would lose my job working for Max. If Namiko couldn't get me back in, I would make Larry's ass regret ever fucking with me and my money.

# MAXIMILIAN

"I'm telling you that she on you man!" Larry said in a frustrated tone.

"I already talked to her about it," I replied shaking my head.

Kiyuki and I had an understanding now. She knew not to push up on me any more. At least I hoped she knew.

"I ain't want to have to tell you this, out of embarrassment, but I see you hard headed as fuck," Larry exhaled. "She called out your name while she was riding my dick," he frowned.

Deshawn and I looked at each other, and burst into laughter. I would've taken that shit to the grave if I were him.

"Wait, this bitch called Max's name out? Were her eyes closed?" Deshawn smiled big as hell and Larry nodded.

"Daaamn! Yo' bitch was fantasizing about another nigga! I wouldn't care though; I would've still busted my nut!" my little brother Konz joked and we laughed.

"Man fuck y'all. You need to fire her bro," Larry spat.

"I ain't firing her because she like me nigga." I shook my head at his petty ass.

"What, you wanna fuck or something?" Larry yelled.

"No, that's just not a good enough reason for me to fire someone," I shrugged.

"Max!" Namiko busted into my office.

"You good ma?" I frowned.

"You need to do something about that bitch, right fucking now!" she yelled.

"Can y'all give us a minute," I told everyone in the room. They paused for a second and then got up to leave. "Now calm down first," I said standing up to walk over to her. "What happened babe?" I finally asked.

"Cori! She threw a fucking brick through my back windshield," she panted heavily. "Either you take care of it or I will. You don't want me to take care of it!" she glared at me.

"Namiko, chill out. I'm gone talk to her," I replied. I stared at her for a couple minutes, admiring how pretty she looked even though her face was all twisted up. She had on an orange dress that matched her dark caramel complexion perfectly. Her long dark hair was in a pony-tail that hung down her back.

"Why are you staring?" she smiled at me surprisingly. I pulled her close, towering over her, and kissed her lips.

"You look so pretty." I bit my lip and she blushed.

"Thank you," she cheesed.

"Let's get a quickie in before I go," I said excitedly as I lifted her onto my desk.

"No Max!" she giggled, as I planted kisses on her sweetly scented neck. I pulled the straps of her dress down, and took her hard nipples into my mouth. "Oohhhh..." she bit her lip, and closed her eyes.

I pulled her panties down, and dropped them on the floor. She unbuckled my pants as we sucked each other's lips, and wrestled with our tongues.

"Shit," I said in a low tone, as I slid into her snug walls.

"Ahhhh uhhhhh," she whimpered, as I slowly pumped into her wetness.

I lifted her smooth legs, and rested them on my forearms for more access. I sped up my pace, as we continued to make love with our mouths at the same time.

"Ahhh! I'm cumming babe!" Namiko yelled as her walls started to contract around my rod.

"Me too ma... fuck," I whispered into her mouth, as I sped up even more. "Fuck!" I called out as I released every bit of me into her. "I'm surprised you're not pregnant," I panted.

"Maybe I am," she smiled.

"What? You are? Why didn't you-"

"I was gonna tell you tonight when you came home, but the whole Cori thing happened," she shrugged and panted.

"So you're having my baby?" I smirked and she nodded her head yes. I wrapped my arms around her small frame, and kissed her passionately as my dick rested inside her. "I love you, ma," I said, looking down into her eyes.

"I love you more Maximilian," she replied in a low tone.

After Namiko and my little session together, I headed over to Cori's. "You been ignoring me and now you show up?" Cori rolled her eyes. She stood in front of me with one thick hip poking out, and her arms folded over her large breasts.

"Why have you been fucking with Namiko?" I asked ignoring her previous comments.

"Nigga please! Only person that gives a fuck about your little Asian persuasion is you!" she spat.

"You telling me you ain't slash her tires, throw a fucking brick through her window, and spray paint her car?" I mugged her, getting irritated by her lies.

"No! I've been worrying about my own fucking life!" She shouted.

"Cori, if you do one more thing to Namiko, I'm gone fuck you up my damn self," I glared down at her.

She looked up at me with glazed eyes. I wasn't gone fall for that crying shit this time though.

"Max, I promise I haven't done anything to her. I love you but it ain't that serious to me." She wiped a single tear from her smooth brown skin. Damn she was a good liar. If I didn't know she had done this shit for sure, I may have believed her. "Please spend some time with me Max," she sniffled, as she wrapped her arms around my torso.

"Cori, I'm married. Stop this shit." I roughly removed her arms from around me. "Don't fuck with Namiko anymore, or you know what's up," I said before quickly exiting.

Did I have more feelings for Cori than I thought? I wasn't sure if it was actually romantic feelings or sympathy. It wasn't anywhere near what I felt for Namiko, whatever it was, but something was there. I was gonna get rid of the feelings ASAP though.

# NAMIKO

Tonight was another exchange. Max wanted to release me because I was his wife, and because I was pregnant with our first child. I liked making my own money though, especially because you never know what events will happen in your life. So just because I had a wealthy husband, didn't mean I was gonna sit at home and not have my own. Shoot, I never expected for my father to become a raging alcoholic, who would attempt to rape me. As I said before, my father was the prototype, and showed no signs of what he soon became, so anything is possible.

I shook those thoughts from my head, as I finished putting my hair into a tight bun. I grabbed my phone to dial Kiyuki, and make sure she was on her way to Red Sugar.

"Hello?" she answered coughing.

"Hey, are you okay?" I frowned.

"I have a little cold. What's up?" she asked like I was bothering her.

"Well, I was just making sure you were on your way to Red Sugar, so we could do the exchange," I said fixing my baby hairs.

"Oh, I'm not feeling well Nami. Tell Max you can do it by yourself. Show him you not a weak bitch," she replied.

"Max knows I'm not weak. I've done an exchange alone before, remember? And did you tell him you weren't coming?"

"Hell no! He wouldn't let me stay home. But you can tell him. You're his wife, he will accept it from you Nami," she coughed.

That had become her favorite line as of late. Whenever she needed some bullshit to be fed to Max, she always wanted me to do it.

"I really think you should talk to him yourself." I shook my head at her as if she could see me.

"Well I don't. Unlike you, Max would fire me. Just tell him I'm sick and that you can do the job alone," she replied matter-of-factly.

"I don't want to do it myself Yuki, I need you to come," I whined.

"Namiko, if you want respect from your man, you need to show him that you're a boss like he is. Why do you think he tried to fuck with me? He knows I'm a boss ass bitch," she said.

"I thought you said you *did* fuck with him? Now you saying he only tried to?" I raised a brow at her delusional ass.

"I did fuck him, but he tried to take our relationship to the next level and I declined. So I fucked him, but I chose not to fuck with him," she laughed. My sister's mental state seemed to be declining by the day.

"Bye Yuki," I replied in a low tone, and disconnected the call.

I swear I wanted to beat her ass so bad. I felt like this job had turned our relationship from sugar to shit. At least I still had Aniku though. I grabbed the rest of my belongings and went over to Red Sugar. I took a deep breath before exiting the car, and then headed up to Max's office.

"Where is Kiyuki ma?" Deshawn asked.

"She's umm... she's sick," I stuttered.

"Sick? This ain't no fucking 9-5 that you can call out of!" Max boomed.

"I know babe, but I can do it," I half smiled, hoping he would allow me to. A part of me felt like Kiyuki was right. I didn't want my husband thinking I was some little weak bitch who couldn't ride for him. I mean, I'd done one alone before, but that was a while ago when we hated one another.

"Who are we gonna send with her?" Deshawn asked. "I can't go, me and Evelyn got a little date," he smirked. Evelyn was fucking with Deshawn heavy ever since Vegas. I smiled inside at the thought.

"I can go alone babe; I-I have done this a bunch of times," I nodded.

"I don't feel safe sending you alone in your state," Max replied in a tone that told me my suggestion wasn't an option.

"Please Max, I don't need anybody. I can go alone, stop acting like I'm weak," I pouted. He stared at me and then shook his head.

"Nah, we can go together," he said standing up and pocketing his keys.

"Max! No!" I yelled and surprised everyone in the room, even myself.

"Namiko! I cannot send you alone with my baby in you! Niggas is crazy!" he yelled back at me.

"Please Max. Let me prove it to you," I smiled seductively. "I always give you what you want," I added and licked my lips.

He paused for a few seconds. "Alright Nami, but no fucking stops. You go straight to the spot, exchange, and then straight back. Matter fact, keep me on the phone the whole time," he replied with his nostrils flaring.

"Okay," I nodded.

I took the folder and the duffle bag, then left to do my job. I was nervous as hell and scared shitless. As soon as I got on the road, I called Max, and put him on speakerphone as I drove. We talked the whole way there, and although I didn't want him on the phone at first, it calmed me that he was somewhat with me.

"Okay, I'm here," I let him know.

Max started to speak, but I hopped out the car to get the product bag. I saw a man standing there, and by the time I got closer, I saw he had a mask on. I was about to turn around, but I heard him cock his gun.

"Give me the shit," he said calmly.

"Please don't do this," I pleaded.

"Just give me the fucking product," he replied sternly. I paused for a couple seconds, until I saw him adjust his grip on the gun. I walked closer, and he snatched the bag from me. "Thanks sexy," he chuckled, and threw the bag into his backseat. He kept the gun pointed at me, until he reached his driver's seat and got in. He then kept his gun pointed out the window, as he sped away.

Once he did, I saw the guy I was supposed to give the product to, laid on the ground in a pool of blood. He had the bag of money laid next to him, except it had been emptied out. I rushed back to the truck, and Max was calling my name frantically.

"Yes, I'm back," I said trying to hide the fact that I was scared as hell.

"How did it go? You got the money?" he asked.

"Max, I-I got robbed again. I-"

"Get back here now!" he yelled cutting me off.

I sped out of the parking lot and back to Red Sugar. Before I pulled up in the parking spot good, Max was storming down the back steps. He rushed over and snatched the driver's side open. After looking me over, he kissed my lips softly. He grabbed my hand and locked the truck, before rushing upstairs to his office.

"You done with this shit Namiko," he said as soon as his office door shut.

"No Max, I -"

"It's over! You not doing this shit no more! You focus on school, our baby, and being my wife! That's it!" he panted with his fists balled up. I knew there was no changing his mind, so I nodded in agreement. "Did you at least see the muthafuckas?" he frowned.

"No," I replied dropping my head.

"Shit!" he said banging his fist on the desk.

"I'm sorry Max." I started to cry. Damn, this baby! I tried to prove myself to him and did the exact opposite.

"Nah baby, this is my fault. I should've gone with you, or at least not let you go at all," he said, shaking his head as he made himself a drink.

"But Max, whomever it was, they were the same person that robbed me last time. I recognized the voice," I said. He turned to me slowly and smiled.

"Good looking out baby," he replied and sipped his scotch. I got up and walked closer to him.

"Are you mad at me?" I asked.

"I couldn't be mad at someone as beautiful as you." He half smiled and squeezed my ass. I rubbed my hand on his beautiful dark caramel face, while admiring his perfect, full lips.

"Well give me a kiss or something to prove it," I finally said.

"I'll give you more than that," he said setting his glass down and picking me up.

"Ah!" I yelped as I wrapped my legs around him, and let him carry me to the couch.

Once we made it, he dipped his tongue in my mouth and proceeded to fuck my brains out.

# KIYUKI

2 months later

None of the shit I was doing had worked the way that I'd wanted it to. I set Namiko up to be robbed again, hoping that Max would get upset with her. I even hoped that he would think she had something to do with the robberies. However, despite my antics, they persevered. Fucking bitches!

I was on my way to visit Cori, because she said she needed to talk. I wanted to talk to her ass too, because she needed to step her shit up with Max. I couldn't do this alone, although I thought I could at first. I'd made Cori think we were the best of friends so I knew she was gonna spill all the beans once I was in front of her.

I pulled up to her apartment, and threw my shit in park. Because I'd made so much money working for Max, I was able to get myself a cute little Mercedes truck.

"What's up ma?" Cori and Deshawn's younger brother Robbie smirked at me.

He was sexy as hell, but too damn young for me. I was twenty-three and he was twenty - not gonna work.

"Hey boo," I smiled back and switched by.

He ran his hand over his fade, and stared at his phone. He and Deshawn looked just alike. They reminded me of Al B Sure's son Quincy.

"Your sister up there?" I asked already knowing the answer. I just wanted to get a good look at his sexy face again.

"Yeah, she up there," he replied, licking his lips.

He didn't do it in a sexual way, but he still looked good as hell when he did it. I put an extra switch in my hips, as I walked up the steps, giving him a nice view of my fat ass.

"Hey," Cori half smiled as she opened her door.

"What's up boo? You look terrible," I commented.

"Thanks for the compliment," she scoffed.

"Anytime. You got something to smoke?" I asked as I sat down on her couch.

"I do," she said, uncovering an ashtray with four pre-rolled blunts in it. I grabbed one out and immediately lit it to get my fix. "So what's been going on?" I asked ready to sip all the tea she was about to serve.

"Well, Max has been tripping on me about fucking with Namiko. I think your sister is fucking with her own shit and blaming me," she exhaled, as she ran her fingers through her hair.

"I could see Namiko doing some shit like that," I nodded. I wanted to laugh so badly, because nobody suspected me of anything.

"Can you? See, I knew it. But Max ain't fucking with me at all. He said if anything else happens to her, he's gonna fuck me up personally," she frowned.

"Damn that's crazy. I thought he loved you," I stated as if I was really concerned.

"Me too, but maybe he likes the skinny hoes now," she shrugged.

Cori was far as hell from skinny. She was thicker than a snicker, had smooth brown skin, with long *real* hair and a pretty smile. She was the real kind of BBW, not the fake ass ones that you see in the music videos.

"I think you need to show him how you feel," I said taking a pull.

"I've tried that Kiyuki," she replied.

"What have you done?" I raised a brow.

"I've begged him for his time. I've sent him naked pictures. I even agreed to still give him some pussy after he told me he married your sister. He denied it then, but when she wasn't giving him none, he texted me on some booty call shit only to stand me up!" she cried.

*Bitch what?* I laughed to myself. There *is* a God. I knew Maximilian was too fucking good to be true. If Cori got him to hit her on some booty call shit *after* being married, I'm sure I could successfully get a booty call or two.

"That ain't enough girl. You got to prove that you down for him. Bring him lunch, shit like that. Act as if *you're* his wife," I nodded.

You see, I wanted Cori to lay it on thick with Max. I knew he would become frustrated with her, and cut her ass off entirely. I wanted Max to completely axe her and be done with her, so that there would be fewer women I had to worry about. I felt bad that I had to do Cori like this, but it was the only way for Max and I to end up together.

Then, Namiko will become frustrated with Cori and the fact that she keeps coming after Max and she will eventually divorce him. He'll be all sad and shit, and mama will be right there to pick up the pieces.

"I feel like that will piss him off," she said.

"Look, I'll let you in on a secret. Namiko got the ring by doing that. She was so thirsty for him, and he eventually fell into the trap," I lied and she smiled.

"Damn, why are you helping me Kiyuki?" she asked.

"Because you deserve him. Just because Namiko is my sister, doesn't mean I would allow her to steal someone's man and be labeled a home wrecker." I shook my head. Cori hugged me tight and almost made me drop my blunt. "Okay, okay," I said nudging her off.

"I really hope this works," she exhaled.

"Oh, it'll work out just fine," I smiled as I blew out smoke. "By the way, can I borrow your car?" I smirked.

# CORI SINEAD

I was definitely gonna take Kiyuki's advice. I mean, she saw first hand how Namiko nabbed Maximilian. So like she said, I was going to act as if *I* was his wife.

Since I was a waitress at Red Sugar, I was around him most of the day. This whole time I'd been giving him his space, because he was trying to be on the good husband tip. But today, all of that was gonna change. Since he liked them thirsty, I was gonna be thirsty as fuck. I made sure my work attire was nice and revealing as it could be. My stomach wasn't flat, so I made sure to cover that up, but my legs were exposed as much as possible. I wore a black cami top, along with some short, tight, black, khaki shorts. I slid on my stilettos and I was ready to go.

"Come in," Max yelled after I knocked on his office door.

"Good evening," I smiled and pushed my long brown hair behind my ears.

"Good evening. You look nice," he commented, as he looked up and down my thick body.

"Thank you. I didn't think you liked them thick anymore," I said as I closed the door behind me.

"You know I love all women. But what's up?" he asked, setting his phone down. Maximilian was fucking gorgeous. He had a dark caramel complexion, lean muscular build, and chocolate brown eyes. He always smelled good and always dressed nice. Whenever you were in his presence, you knew you were around a boss ass nigga. I had to have him, and not even a wife was gonna stop me from obtaining him.

"I just wanted to chit-chat before my shift. Plus, I made you some food." I smiled and held up the brown paper bag.

"Oh word? What is it?" he smiled big.

"Grilled pork chops, mashed potatoes, applesauce, and cream spinach. It's your favorite meal." I licked my lips and walked it over to his desk.

"Damn ma, thank you," he nodded as he looked into the bag.

"Does your wife make that for you?" I raised an eyebrow.

"She has, yes," he replied, shocking me. "But she has never brought it to work for me, so thank you," he added when he realized I was bothered by his answer.

"Oh." I smiled and sat on the edge of his desk. "So how is it being married?" I asked.

"It's straight. I actually like it, especially cause we're having a baby," he smiled, almost to himself.

"You're having a baby?" my voice cracked.

"Yeah," he replied.

I felt like I was about to have a heart attack. I didn't want him to have a family with her. He and I were supposed to be a family. I didn't know if I could deal with the fact that she would be having his first child.

"Max, I'm gonna keep it real with you. I'm so in love with you and... I just want us to be an 'us' again. How we were before Namiko," I smiled.

"How were we before Namiko? Because I remember that we stopped fucking around about two months before I met her," he frowned in confusion.

"Yeah, because you said you didn't want anything serious. When you did want something more serious, I assumed you would hit me up, not move on to a completely different girl," I spat, feeling myself become upset.

"Cori, let's be honest here. You and I never connected like that. It was always on some fuck buddy shit. I need a woman I can talk to. I need my woman to be my best friend," he said.

"I tried to talk! But every time you got in my presence you were bending me over!" I yelled standing up.

"Yo, calm the fuck down! Regardless of what we had or didn't have, I'm off the market so it really doesn't matter," he shrugged.

"Will you still be off the market once your wife finds out you agreed to still give me a chance, the day after your wedding? Will you be off the market once she sees all the texts you were still sending me that week she wouldn't give you no pussy?" I asked placing my hand on my hip.

"Oh, you trying to blackmail me or something? Yeah, I may have pressed up on you but guess what? It was just for some pussy as usual. Only reason I ever contact you is for some pussy. And when's the last time I even hit you up? Oh right, that period where Namiko wasn't giving it up. And even then, when you told me to come through I never did," he shrugged.

Each word he spoke stabbed me in the heart. I tired to make myself believe that we'd had a deeper connection all this time, but he was right. All he'd ever talked to me for was to get between my legs. We never stayed up talking all night. When he tried to talk to me, I never had anything to say. Our small talk would soon turn to awkward silence, or me groping his dick to make up for our lack of an intellectual connection. It'd kept him in the past, so why not try it now? I walked over and attempted to straddle his lap slowly.

"Back yo' ass up," he said stopping me. "You just tried to blackmail me, and now you want some dick? Take your bipolar ass on somewhere before I fire your ass," he said flaring his nostrils.

"If I leave Max, I don't want you to ever contact me again," I said, not meaning a word of it. I was just talking out my ass by this point. This whole encounter had gone to the left ever since the mention of his baby on the way.

"I'm giving you five seconds to leave before I terminate you," he reiterated.

I nodded my head and quickly left before the tears fell.

**Me:** *I think it's really over Kiyuki.*
**Kiyuki:** *you and Max?*
**Me:** *yeah who else?*
I frowned at my phone.
**Kiyuki:** *About time he stuck with one woman.*
I read her text and didn't respond, because she was acting weird. I went to the bathroom to fix my face, and proceeded to finish my shift. I was too good of a woman to keep chasing behind Max. Soon as little miss Namiko shut her legs for a month again, he'd be crawling back. Once that happened, I'd be having his baby too.

# NAMIKO

I was leaving my political science class, feeling like shit. This baby made me feel hungry and groggy all the damn time. All I wanted to do was go get some fast food and go home to wait for Max. I was getting used to him rubbing my stomach until I fell asleep. I was only three months, and nothing was really showing, but it still felt good.

After walking a distance that felt like ten miles, I finally made it my car. As I was putting my backpack and purse in the backseat, a black Ford Explorer pulled up to my car. I looked towards it, and was met with a bucket of ice-cold coffee grounds. As I screamed and tried to wipe the shit out of my eyes, I heard the car speed off, but not before a female yelled to leave her man alone.

"Here is some water, let me flush your eyes," some girl said. I paused and let her rinse some of the coffee grounds from my eyes with her bottle of water. "Is that better?" she smiled.

"Yeah, thank you," I replied breathing heavily.

"You're welcome. I'm Claudia," she smiled and stuck her hand out.

"I would but my hands are a mess. Nice to meet you though Claudia," I half smiled.

"Likewise," she replied and walked off.

I looked down over my clothes, and saw I was drenched form head to toe in wet coffee grounds. I got into my car, not even caring about the mess I was making, and sped to Red Sugar. As soon as I walked in, I spotted Gordon the manager, and headed over to him.

"Is Cori here?" I asked.

"It's her day off ma. Why? What happened to you?" he asked.

That was all the confirmation I needed to know it was Cori who did this shit. I left back out without answering Gordon's question, and sped to Cori's house. As soon as I arrived, I ran to her door and knocked like I was the police.

"What bitch!" she yelled as she flung open the door. I cocked my fist back, and punched her so hard that she stumbled back into her heater.

"What the fuck is going on?" her brother Robbie questioned, as he ran up her steps.

I ignored him and charged that bitch. I delivered one blow after the other to her face, and the blood flying in my face didn't stop me. I was tired of this bitch fucking with me. She grabbed a handful of my hair, but I kept the punches coming so she couldn't do much.

"Chill the fuck out!" her brother yelled, as he yanked me away from her while she pulled out pieces of my hair.

"I'm gonna kill you!" she yelled holding my real hair strands in her hand.

"Do it now bitch!" I hollered back, waving her towards me as Robbie carried me outside and to my car. There was a crowd of nosey ass ghetto neighbors, watching closely.

"Get the fuck out of here," he panted as he put me down on my feet.

I stared up at her, as she glared down at me over her balcony. After a couple seconds, I went ahead and got into my car. I was ready for my next victim, Maximilian Davis. I told him to take care of this bitch, and clearly he couldn't.

I raced through the streets of Detroit, until I finally arrived back at Red Sugar. I rushed inside and to Max's office. I frantically twisted on the doorknob of his office and saw it was locked. Lord for his sake, he better not be in here with another bitch. I silently prayed for him. I was in another state of mind right now, and I would kill both of their asses right here with all these witnesses.

"Open this fucking door nigga!" I yelled as I banged on his wooden door with my fist. I kept switching back and forth between banging on the door and twisting the knob until it finally flew open. "You better not have a bitch in here!" I shouted as I stormed in, shoulder checking Max in the process. I saw the room was filled with his team, so he was lucky. "Tell everybody to get the fuck out unless you want them in your business!" I spat and folded my arms.

"Namiko, this is not a good time ma," Max replied nonchalantly. Oh this nigga thought I was fucking playing?

"Fine. I'm leaving your bitch ass since you can't control your fucking hoes! Do you see me right now? Yeah, this is courtesy of your little hoe on the side! But she can have yo' ass cause I'm done!" I said throwing my rings at him. "Oh, and I'm getting an abortion," I lied. I wasn't killing my baby over his weak ass. Plus, I don't even think I could get one this late.

"Namiko- everyone excuse us please," Max finally replied.

His face was full of anger, but I didn't care. I was ready to box with his ass, so he better calm that ass down. Everyone quickly exited, and I stood there with a smug expression.

"You ain't killing shit!" he said through gritted teeth, a couple seconds after the last person left. "Don't you ever bring your ignorant ass up in my shit acting like a fucking hood rat ever again, or I will knock your fucking lights out!" he continued. His anger and aggressiveness was sexy as hell, but this was not the time.

"Don't worry about me being a hood rat. Worry about the divorce we're about to get, and your new bitch. She might need you since I just came from whooping her ass," I said.

"Yeah, maybe I should go check on her," he smirked.

I couldn't help myself and started to take off on his ass. Once my fist finally connected with his nose, he grabbed my wrists and pinned them down.

"Namiko, I don't hit women but you about to take me there," he panted, as he gripped my wrists tightly.

"I hate you! I fucking hate you! You played me this whole fucking time!" I cried. I was so upset that I let him see how much he hurt me.

"Shut the fuck up with that shit! Ain't nobody fucking played you! You know I love yo' crazy ass! That baby got your emotions all over the place!" he spat.

"Let me go Max. I'm tired of looking at you," I replied calmly.

"I'm gone let you go, but keep your hands to yourself," he panted.

"Nigga, get off me!" I snatched away from him and stormed out.

Once I got outside, I took a big rock that was lying on the floor of the parking lot, and lunged it through Max's back windshield.

I didn't know what the hell was wrong with me. I'd never been this angry in my life. I think the baby was making me a crazy person.

"Namiko, what the fuck!" Max yelled as he ran over to his car.

"Fuck you, nigga!" I screamed as I unlocked my car.

"Woman, you better be glad I'm crazy about you and you're carrying my baby. Otherwise I would pump two in your fucking dome right now!" he shouted as he inspected his busted window.

I ignored him and cranked my car up. I sped out the lot almost hitting him on purpose, and then headed to my old home I shared with my sisters.

# MAXIMILIAN

2 weeks later

Namiko and I had been distant for a couple weeks, and it was killing me. I tried talking to her after what I felt like was enough time for her to calm down, but she seemed to be more upset than before. I didn't know what to do. I approached Cori and she swore up and down she didn't do that shit. If she wasn't my best friend's sister, I would've been murked her ass.

I was trying to keep tabs on Namiko, because I didn't want her getting an abortion. I was happy to know that she was going to class and then home, no doctor's offices or clinics.

I was chilling in my theatre room, when I heard the doorbell ring. *I really need a maid,* I said to myself, as I got up to answer the door. No one knew where I lived, so I felt comfortable enough to answer my own shit. "Who is it?" I called out.

"Kiyuki." I frowned out of irritation, and then pulled the door open.

"What's good?" I asked.

"I just came to get some of Namiko's things," she smirked. I bet she was jumping for joy at the fact that her sister and I were separated.

"Aight. Hurry up though, 'cause I have somewhere to be," I said. I didn't have anywhere to be, but I didn't want her in my crib.

I showed her the bedroom so she could pack Namiko's stuff, and then sat on the bed to supervise. Kiyuki was grimy and I knew she might try to pocket some of my shit if I left her alone.

"Damn nigga, you don't trust me?" she asked once she realized I'd made myself comfortable in the room.

"Nope," I replied dryly.

She smiled seductively, and then bent over to unzip the suitcase. Her fat ass was very tempting, but not tempting enough. I grabbed a magazine to sit in my lap, when I saw my dick start to harden.

"It's hot," she exhaled and removed her sweatshirt. She had nothing but a bra on under, and I scoffed. Who wears only a bra under their sweatshirt? Hoes do. "Why is it so hot?" she asked turning to me. Her nipples were poking through her silk bra, and her stomach was nice and toned like Namiko's. Well like Namiko's used to be, she had a slight bulge now.

"I don't know, but hurry up," I ordered.

"Fine." She turned her lip up and began packing again.

**Me:** *Why did you send your sister? You scared of daddy? Lol*

**Mrs. Davis:** *Fuck you.*

**Me:** *Lmao. I love you too baby mama.*

That baby had turned Namiko into a whole new person. She was never this feisty, and it kind of turned me on. I liked the switch just as much as I loved the sweet Namiko. I loved everything about her and I didn't care how she acted. I wanted her in anyway that she came, whether she was sweet or spicy.

**Me:** *When you gone let daddy taste it again?*

**Mrs. Davis:** *Never, this is someone else's pussy now.*

**Me:** *Yeah right. It's gone always be mine. It's only gonna feel my dick, and only push out my babies. I'm thinking about how hard you cum for me right now.*

**Mrs. Davis:** *Leave me alone Maximilian.*

I laughed at her response, and put my phone away.

"Is something funny?" Kiyuki frowned.

"Just joking with the wife," I smirked.

"I see," she said zipping up the suitcase. "I'm gonna use the bathroom before I go," she said, pointing to the restroom within my bedroom.

I nodded and picked up my phone to respond to some texts. After about five minutes, she exited the bathroom butt ass naked.

"Hey Max," she smirked as she sashayed over to me. Her body was nothing short of perfection, and she knew that shit. I swear she and her sisters were putting Blasians on the map.

"Go put your damn clothes on Kyuki," I exhaled.

"You and Nami aren't even together anymore. This is your chance to try it out." She smiled as she placed one leg on the chair in our room.

She slid her fingers along the slit of her pussy, as she licked her lips. *Damn, damn, damn.*

"I'm not interested in trying out some shit every nigga in Detroit has tried," I replied.

"Nigga please, this pussy is exclusive. Not anybody can get it. You don't want to pass this up," she said as she sat down in the chair.

She lifted her legs and spread them wide. She took two fingers and slipped them inside her hole. She plunged them in and out, as she stared at me biting her lip. I stood up and walked over to her, causing a smile to spread across her face.

"Mmmm, I knew you would come around," she said as she sped up her motions. I grabbed her by the arm and yanked her off the chair.

"Put your fucking clothes on and go," I said through gritted teeth. She glared at me, and then stormed over to get dressed. "Wash your fucking hands before touching my door knobs," I added.

She washed her hands in the bathroom, and then grabbed the suitcase full of Namiko's clothes. She stared me down one last time, but I pretended not to see her. She grunted, and then left the bedroom. I followed after her to make sure she left.

*Good job Max*, I said to myself, and then headed to the den to make myself a drink. Passing up that pussy showed me I'd come along way. It also showed me how much I loved my crazy, hormonal wife.

# KIYUKI

"Ride that dick." Jared bit his lip as he gripped my waist.

"Fuck," I moaned as I felt myself about to cum.

He smacked my ass and gripped my butt cheeks roughly. I bounced harder and faster, until we both released together.

"Damn, you got some fire. If you weren't such a hoe, I probably would wife you," he joked, as I plopped down next to him.

"Please negro, you ain't got enough bread to wife a bitch like me." I rolled my eyes.

"Well ever since I robbed ya brother-in-law, I been doing much better and so have you." He laughed and took a pull on a blunt.

"What time is it?" I asked no one in particular, as I picked up my phone. "Three o'clock in the afternoon, I have to go," I said, getting up and lightly jogging to his bathroom. I cleaned myself up, and then went back to the bedroom to get dressed.

"Damn, you just came for some dick and that's it?" Jared frowned.

"Oh, and to make sure you know what to say if you get caught." I raised a brow as I buttoned my jeans.

"Who do I say sent me? Claire?" he joked, flashing his sexy ass smile.

"Cori nigga," I replied shaking my head. "Aight, I have to go," I said as I kissed his lips lightly.

I sped home because I wanted to be there when Namiko got home from class. Ever since Max blew me off and kicked me out his house, I'd been on a mission to push Namiko to file for a divorce. At first I just wanted to separate them, but since he didn't want to fuck with me, I was gone have them split up legally and permanently.

"Hey Yuki," Namiko said as she walked through the door with her stupid ass friend Evelyn.

"What's up? How are you feeling?" I asked like I cared.

"I'm not as sick anymore, but I'm still eating a lot," she and Evelyn laughed.

I fake laughed with them, and rolled my eyes at Evelyn when her back was turned. I never liked her ass, because she was always trying to be Namiko's bodyguard. You couldn't say shit to Namiko without her trying to step her ugly ass in.

"Sit Nami, I want to talk to you," I said patting the couch cushion next to me.

Evelyn smacked her lips and sat in the La-Z-Boy chair adjacent to us. *Ignore her Kiyuki*, I told myself.

"What's up?" Namiko asked as she sat next to me.

"I think you should go ahead and divorce Max," I nodded.

"Already? I wanted to think about it for a little bit," she frowned.

"She probably wants to marry him herself," Evelyn chimed in.

"Can you mind your business please?" I spat at Evelyn.

"Anything that has something to do with Namiko *is* my business," she replied, cocking her head to the left. I rolled my eyes and diverted my attention back to my sister.

"He was fucking with Cori the whole time," I said to Namiko.

"He was? I don't believe that," she replied shaking her head.

"Cause she lying," Evelyn chuckled.

"Okay, I have proof Nami," I said pulling out my phone.

I showed her the texts of when Cori said it was finally over. I'm sure she wondered why I was replying in such an odd way that day, but this was all a part of the plan. Namiko's eyes started to glaze over, as she took forever to read the short conversation.

"Let me see Nami," Evelyn said. Didn't this bitch have something better to do? I thought she was fucking with Deshawn.

Namiko handed Evelyn my phone, and she read the texts then smacked her lips. "Why is she venting to you anyway? You supposed to be on Namiko's side," Evelyn inquired suspiciously.

"Because I told Nami from the beginning that he was taken. I don't want my sister being labeled as a home wrecker, or thinking I support her ways, so I let Cori know that," I lied, and snatched my phone from Evelyn.

"Namiko, don't get a divorce unless you want one," Evelyn said.

"I know I-"

"No! You need to get one! Stop being so damn weak! Do you need more coffee grounds thrown on you?" I yelled.

I'd paid a friend of mine to throw that shit on Namiko. I couldn't do it myself, because she would've recognized my car and voice. I made sure my home girl used Cori's car though.

"I'll start the process," Namiko said dropping her head.

"Nami! Stop letting her think for you!" Evelyn frowned.

"Bitch I'm getting real tired of you! Namiko is *my* sister! Why are you always in her business? You probably want to eat her pussy!" I spat.

"Just like you want to suck Max's dick! Namiko, she is jealous, don't fall for it," Evelyn glared at me.

"Ain't nobody jealous! I'm doing what's best for my sister!" I yelled.

"Are you? Cause you sound like a fucking hater to me! You've always been jealous of Namiko!" she said standing up like she wanted to fight. I stood up as well, and walked over to her. "Get out my face Yuki, or we gone have a problem," she threatened me.

"Nope," I smirked, and she swung. I caught her wrist before it connected with my jaw, and prepared to hit her ass.

"Stop y'all! Damn! I'm gonna do what I want no matter what! Regardless of what either one of y'all say!" Namiko shouted and left to her room.

Evelyn snatched her wrist from me and followed after her. As soon as that bitch left, I was gonna make sure I convinced Namiko to divorce Max.

# NAMIKO

A Couple Weeks Later...

Today I was going over to the house I shared with my soon to be ex-husband, so I could discuss the divorce. He'd finally stopped texting and calling me, and Kiyuki said it was probably because he had a new woman in his life. I cried at first, but then I decided it was time to move on.

He told me to come over today, and I just knew he was going to ask for a divorce as well. I rubbed my stomach that was barely there, and then walked up the steps to ring the doorbell.

"Good evening," a young lady answered. I tensed up until I saw she was wearing a maid's outfit.

"Hi, I am here to see Maximilian. Is he here?" I half smiled.

"What is your name?" she smiled. "Namiko Davis. I mean Allen. Namiko Allen." I corrected myself because I needed to get used to using my maiden name again.

"Oh yes, Mrs. Da-Allen. Come in. I'm Zelda," she smiled and waved me in. I walked into my old home, and immediately missed being here and being with Max. "He's in the bedroom, did you need me to show you to it?" she smiled.

"No. Thank you Zelda," I half smiled. She nodded and walked away.

I slowly walked up the stairs, and it felt like I was walking to my death. I was scared that he'd called me over here to officially break it off. Why was I scared when that's what I was going to tell him as well? I should be happy that both parts would want the split. Then again, both parts wouldn't want it.

I didn't want a divorce from Max, but I had to divorce him after all that he'd done. Kiyuki showed me the texts he'd sent to Cori that week I withheld sex, and then the fact that he'd slept with her the day after we got married. I just couldn't stay. What would that look like? What kind of example would I be setting for the child in my stomach?

I finally reached the bedroom door and slowly twisted the knob. Max was looking through some clothes, wearing socks and sweats only. His abs, arms, and back looked so strong. Would it be bad to have some going away sex?

"Hello," I finally spoke up.

He turned around to me, and Lord I almost forgot how gorgeous he was. He smiled and walked towards me, looking so damn fine that my breathing became heavy. I had on some thin sweat shorts, and I felt like they would be soon soaked in the crotch. My nipples were poking through my camisole, and I was embarrassed.

"Hey babe," he finally replied once he neared and towered over me.

"W-what did you want to talk about?" I stammered slightly. *Get it together Namiko!* I told myself.

"Oh, it's time for you to come home," he said sternly.

"What?" I frowned in confusion.

"Yeah, this whole time away has been going on long enough. So it's time to come back here with your man," he rephrased.

"I don't want to!" I lied. I was so dramatic.

"Oh you don't?" he smirked and softly pecked my lips.

"No," I whispered as he continued to kiss me.

I cupped his smooth face, as he tongued me down and sucked my lips. He removed my jacket as he backed me to the bed.

"Wait Max, you cheated the day after we were married and when I wouldn't have sex with you that week," I said placing a hand on his rock hard chest.

"I never cheated on you," he panted as he kissed my neck and collarbone. "I would never cheat on you," he whispered in-between kisses.

"What about the day after we were married?" I quizzed.

"I almost did, but I caught myself. Plus, that was a long time ago babe," he exhaled.

"No, I have to go. I only came to tell you I want a divorce," I said, turning to leave as the tears spilled out. He grabbed me from behind and lifted my camisole off. "No," I cried as he unsnapped my bra, and reached around to cup my small breasts.

He kissed the nape of my neck, as he played with my nipples. He then ran one hand down the front of my body, and into my panties. He started to play with my clit, while still massaging my nipple and kissing my shoulders. He was like a well-oiled machine.

"Ahhh," I purred as he brought me to an orgasm. He turned me to face him, and pressed his lips against mine. "I can't come back to you," I whispered as he pushed down my panties and shorts.

"Why not? I'm your husband," he replied in-between kisses.

"I'm setting a bad example for the baby," I said as he laid my naked body on the bed.

"You're setting a bad example if you leave me. I love you baby. We need to stay together forever. That's setting a good example," he said, and then started to kiss down my stomach. He paused at my mid section for a bit, recognizing the growing life inside me. "I had a moment of weakness that I didn't even act on. Something I would never act on. Don't leave your baby's daddy, your husband," he whispered before taking my clit into his mouth.

"Max, ahhhh," I moaned. He sucked softly yet strongly, as he pushed my legs back towards me. He dipped his tongue into my hole, and played with my swollen clit until I came again.

"You staying?" he asked as he took my nipple into his mouth. I shook my head yes, as I watched him. "You gone stick by me forever?" he questioned as he switched back and forth between nipples.

"Yes," I whispered as my opening throbbed in anticipation. I'd been so horny these past few weeks, and only getting by off the memories of he and I.

"Promise me," he said now staring down into my eyes, with his thick head positioned at my opening. He started to push his way inside me, while keeping his eyes locked with mine. "Promise me," he repeated as he stroked me slowly.

"I promise baby," I whimpered, feeling him in my stomach damn near. I missed him so much.

"Good girl," he replied before hungrily dipping his tongue in my mouth.

# MAXIMILIAN

"What's the fucking hold up Larry!" I yelled.

"Man, I'm working on it," he exhaled.

"What the fuck do I need you for, when you taking so damn long to find out who did this shit?" I frowned.

This nigga was supposed to be looking into who'd robbed Namiko those two times, and he was still empty handed. Now here I was about to find out for my damn self. I had changed the route so the person wasn't able to rob the new chicks, Claudia and Aubrey that I'd hired.

Tonight, Deshawn and I were going on the old route just to see if we would get held up. We had no product or money on us of course, but we just needed to catch this nigga.

"I'm gone do it man. Let me come with y'all tonight," Larry pleaded.

"Nah, you can't fucking come with us tonight homie. This what you should've done already." Deshawn shook his head as he stood up.

"Aye nigga, I was talking to Max, not you!" Larry spat.

"It don't matter. You fired as of now nigga. Be gone," I cut in.

"Damn, over this one little thing?" he frowned.

"One little thing? Nigga, do you know how much product, and ultimately money I lost? Do you know how many enemies I've made, because the person who was killed while picking up the product, peoples think I set them up? Man, get the fuck out my face before I blast yo' fucking head open," I said glaring at him. I was ready to whoop his ass.

"Aight. Bet," Larry nodded and then left. Deshawn and I headed down to the truck and then got on the road.

"Man, I hope we catch this nigga," I exhaled.

"Me too. They getting murked on sight. Larry is lucky he alive," Deshawn replied, lighting a blunt.

"I know right," I nodded.

I spotted the gas station that Namiko was robbed at, and decided to stop there, just to see if the person would repeat their actions there. I went into the store and shopped for some candies and juice that I didn't really want, as I watched the truck intently. Nothing. I paid for the shit I picked out, and then jogged back to the car.

"Damnit," I said once I entered the car.

"Let's go to the exchange location and see if that's the bait spot," Deshawn suggested.

I nodded and started the car, but as I was driving away, Deshawn stopped me and let me know my door wasn't shut all the way. I stopped and opened the door, and then bingo, a nigga ran up on me with a gun.

"Gimme that work!" he yelled.

I saw his hand was trembling, and I smirked. I guess his bitch ass was only used to robbing women. I hopped out the car, and he backed up a little, while still aiming the gun at me. I held my hands up in mock surrender, as I neared him.

"You the one been robbing my shit I see." I chuckled and saw Deshawn run around to the driver's side where we were.

I then quickly snatched the gun from his trembling hand. He tried to run, but I busted a cap in the back of his knee. He continued to limp away, but finally collapsed. The gas station attendant ran outside frantically, looking around, like a chicken with its head cut off. I had no choice but to kill his ass since he was a witness. Deshawn ran inside to collect the camera footage, as I dragged the stick up kid to my truck. I snatched his mask off, and saw I didn't recognize his ass. Deshawn finally came running out with a gang of camera tapes, and we sped off. We stopped in a dark area, and then shut the engine off.

"Who you working with, Larry?" I asked turning to the groaning nigga in my backseat.

"Cori," he panted.

"Cori? Nigga what?" Deshawn frowned looking the nigga up and down.

"Cori. Thick brown-skinned bitch. Tssstttt," he said rocking back and forth, holding his knee.

Deshawn and I looked at each other and I shook my head. I put my silencer on, and emptied two shots into the nigga's head.

After getting rid of his body, Deshawn and I sat in my office in silence. "Man, I don't believe Cori did this shit," he said rubbing a hand over his fade.

"The nigga said it D! How else would he know her?" I frowned in irritation.

"I don't know man. But damn, why would she do this?" he asked, throwing his hands out in front of him.

"I ain't sure, but you need to figure that shit out. I'm only sparing her life cause she yo' sister, but if another robbery occurs, she's gone," I said sternly and he nodded.

☙❦❧

"Ahhh Max," Namiko cried out, as I pumped into her fast and hard. I admit I was taking my frustrations out on the pussy, but it was feeling too good to stop.

"Fuck Nami. Shit," I grunted out of breath. I had her legs on my shoulders, as I stared down at her small sexy body. Her sex faces made my dick harder, and I busted earlier than I wanted to. "Fuckkk," I groaned as I released. I let her legs down and she pulled me close. I groped her sweaty body, while licking her face. We sucked each other's lips until my dick got hard again.

# KIYUKI

I'd heard that Maximilian had fired Larry, and I knew we would now have an enemy in common. Although he and I hadn't talked in forever, since I called out Max's name during sex, I knew he'd be down to plot against his former boss. Larry was a hating ass nigga, so he wouldn't be able to stand by and watch Max get money after firing him.

"Fuck you doing here?" He stared at me with a scowl on his face.

"I missed you," I said reaching over to touch him. He slapped my hand away, which caught me off guard.

I was only over here because I knew Jared was dead. Being greedy finally caught up with his dumb ass. I told him to only go when I told him to, but no he had to do his own thing. Max fired me after I tried to get him to fuck me, so my money was drying up.

"So I heard what happened babe," I said looking over at him.

"Happened when?" he asked dryly.

"I know Max fired you. He fired me too," I said hoping to bond with him.

"He fired me for no damn reason, he fired you cause you're a hoe," he chuckled.

"Whatever, he pressed up on me so many times it's ridiculous." I shook my head.

"What you mean?" he frowned.

"He's been fucking me this whole time Larry! When I tried to break it off, he fired me," I whined, as if I was a damsel in distress. If he believed this bullshit I was feeding him, his ass was dumber than he looked - and he looked hella dumb!

"No wonder he was refusing to fire yo' ass at first!" he yelled, and I nodded, although I didn't know what he was talking about.

"I only called his name during sex because I was so used to being with him." I added fuel to the fire.

"I knew something was up. The whole time he was fucking my girl!" he scoffed. "Why did you even do it?" he asked. Think fast Kiyuki.

"Because he said if I wanted to work for him, I needed to give him what he wanted," I lied.

"Greedy ass nigga." He shook his head in disgust. "You know I would've looked out for you though," he replied confused.

"You know I like having my own Lawrence," I said. "But let's get this nigga. Let's rob and kill him." I smiled and hoped he went along with it.

"How?" he questioned.

"I don't know. You know how he moves better than I do." I smiled seductively and ran a finger along the back of his neck.

"What you gone do for me?" he bit his lip.

I got down on the floor, and unzipped his pants to release his dick. I took all of him in my mouth, which wasn't much, and bobbed up and down slowly.

"Fuck," he moaned in a low tone. I took his balls into my mouth as well, and used my saliva to jack him off at the same time. "I'm 'bout to nut Yuki," he grunted loudly, with his minute ready rice ass. "Arrgggh-hhhhh!" he called out as his seeds spilled down my throat.

I usually would've moved prior to him busting, but I needed him on my side. He caressed the back of my head, and played with my hair as he leaned his head back.

"Let's get this nigga," he smirked.

After chopping it up and planning with Larry on how to get at Max, I headed home. I was tired because of all this scheming I'd been doing. Cori had been blowing me up, but I didn't have time for her ass. She and I were no longer friends, now that I'd gotten what I needed out of her. I laughed as I pulled into my driveway.

I saw Namiko's new car parked in the driveway, and rolled my eyes. I walked by her Range Rover and purposely bumped it with my Louis bag. Hopefully, it scratched something.

"Where you been?" my baby sister Aniku frowned.

"Handling my own business, something you should do," I joked and headed to the back.

"What are you doing?" I asked Namiko as I leaned in her doorway.

"I'm taking all my stuff," she smiled.

"Oh yeah, I forgot Max took your backbone out. Already running back," I laughed, although I was irritated.

"Call it what you want Yuki. I owe it to our baby and our marriage to try and work it out," she replied without looking at me.

"I forgot you were pregnant," I spoke honestly.

It had totally slipped my mind that she had hit the jackpot and gotten pregnant by none other than Maximilian Davis. I shook my head out of irritation when her back was to me.

"Well I haven't forgotten. All I do is eat, and I have definitely gained weight," she chuckled.

"Good thing Max loves the big girls too," I spat referring to Cori. I wanted to remind her of her husband's *alleged* extramarital affairs.

"Yep," she simply replied.

"Well good luck weakling," I joked before turning around.

"I feel bad for you," she said calmly.

"Bad for me?" I raised a brow and turned back around to face her.

"Yeah, you're so miserable that all you do is try to bring others down," she scoffed.

"Ain't nobody tryna bring your naive ass down! I'm trying to point out to you that your husband is a dog!" I yelled making our little sister Aniku appear.

Honestly, I was more upset that Max *wasn't* dogging her out. As time went by, I was starting to see that he really did love my sister.

"What's going on?" Aniku asked.

"Well listen Kiyuki, I like dogs. Love them actually. And I love me some Maximilian Davis too. If I need your input or advice, I will ask for it. Otherwise, please work on your own issues, like figuring out where you're gonna live now that you have no job," she fake-smiled.

"So you're just gonna leave Aniku here? You should pay the mortgage for her at least," I folded my arms.

"Nami asked me to come live with her and Max, so I'm leaving with her tonight," Aniku said, looking at me with a concerned expression.

"Wow! So fuck me? After all I've done for y'all? Especially you! You fucking murderer," I said glaring at Namiko.

"Come on Aniku," she said ignoring my threat. Aniku stared at me for a couple seconds, and then grabbed her bag to leave with Namiko.

"Fuck!" I yelled punching the wall.

It was cool though, because soon enough she would be a widow, and I would have my cash. But just because she wanted to jump bad with me, I would make sure to get rid of that baby she was carrying first. I smirked and then headed to my bedroom to sleep peacefully.

# NAMIKO

niku and I were out to dinner at Olive Garden in Dearborn, just so that we could spend some time together. I'd been so caught up in my life with Max, that I felt like our relationship had become somewhat distant. But ever since she moved in, things had been on their way back to normal, thank God. Whenever Max was gone all day, she would keep me company, and I had almost forgotten how much I'd missed her little cute self.

We'd already been shopping earlier, courtesy of Max, so dinner was the perfect way to end the day.

"I am so full." I smiled and rubbed my growing stomach, as I stood up from the table.

"What? I thought I'd never hear that," Aniku chuckled, as we headed towards the door.

"Shut up," I said rolling my eyes.

As we walked through the semi-dark parking lot, I saw a group of girls standing by my car.

"Who the fuck are they?" Aniku asked.

They were staring me down with scowls on their faces, wearing tennis shoes, camis, and tights. Aniku and I stopped in our tracks to get some time to think. I had no problem getting down with these bitches, but it was five of them and I was pregnant. I grabbed Aniku's hand and walked back into the restaurant. We went into the bathroom, and I pulled out my phone to dial Max as she locked the door.

"Hey babe," he answered.

"Either you got some other hoes I don't know about that's out here waiting on me, or Cori sent them," I said in a low tone.

"What? What are you talking about?" he inquired.

"It's five bitches waiting by my car, outside of the Olive Garden on Ford Max. They're standing there looking at me with an attitude. They're ready to fight," I said getting annoyed.

"Okay, stay inside for a little bit and see if they leave. I'm gonna come through."

"Fine," I replied shaking my head, as Aniku stared at me with her eyes bucked.

"Aye, and just so you know, I ain't been fucking with no bitches so get that shit out of your head," he added.

"I know," I smiled and we disconnected.

Aniku and I walked back through the restaurant, and looked out the window. The girls were still waiting there, but now they were looking on their phones and conversing with one another.

"Fuck this shit. Let's go," I said to Aniku.

"You sure Nami? You're pregnant," Aniku frowned.

"You can stay here, and I will go out there," I said, and she nodded nervously.

I took a deep breath and slowly headed over to my car. "Can I help you guys?" I asked and they stopped talking and put their phones away.

"Yeah, you seem to not be able to stay away from Max," the front-runner said.

"That's my husband, why would I stay away from him?" I asked cocking my head to the right.

"Because he's taken, but we understand that a hoe like you doesn't care about that," she smiled and her girls snickered.

"You hear how dumb you sound? He's married to me, yet you're saying he's taken by someone else. That's impossible honey," I fake-smiled.

She walked up to me and shoved me back hard as fuck. Then

another girl pushed me to the left, and then another girl shoved me to the right. They continued pushing me in all kinds of directions, as the last two girls laughed.

"Ladies, I'm pregnant! Stop!" I yelled as I flew in all kinds of directions. As soon as the words left my mouth, the ringleader punched me in the face.

"Nami!" I heard Aniku yell as she rushed over.

"Go back inside Aniku!" I shouted back as I touched my lip for blood.

I charged the ringleader, and started taking off on her ass. I was fucking her up until her friend yanked me back by my hair. Another girl karate kicked me in the stomach, and all I thought about was my baby. I saw Aniku run up on the girl who kicked me and they started to fight. I collapsed to the ground as I groaned in pain. The ringleader straddled me and punched me continuously until I passed out.

# MAXIMILIAN

eshawn and I were leaving the hospital from visiting my baby Namiko. That shit was fucking me up seeing her laid up like that, but I needed to be strong for her. The chicks who jumped her said they were sent by Cori, and despite what Deshawn wanted, I needed that bitch dead.

"I can't do this blind eye shit no more D. Your sister has crossed the fucking line!" I said to Deshawn once we got into the car.

"Man, I talked to her and she said she ain't have nothing to do with this shit, nor the robberies," he frowned. I hated to put him in this situation, because I knew he had loyalty to both of us.

"But how would all these people know Cori dawg?" I frowned as I stared out the window.

"Shit, just let me talk to her again," he suggested and blew out hot air.

"Nah, I'm coming with you this time," I nodded.

"That's fine, but let's get all the facts first," he said and I agreed.

We drove down to Cori's apartment, and when we got there, her black Ford Explorer was parked outside. Her brother Robbie was outside as well, smoking a cigarette until we got his attention.

"Why you bringing this nigga over here?" Robbie asked Deshawn as he glared at me.

"I wasn't aware that we had a problem little nigga," I said glaring back.

"Yeah we do. I don't appreciate you dogging my sister out bruh," he said walking closer to me like he wanted to do something.

"Deshawn, you better get your little brother if you want him to live," I smirked, as we stared each other down.

"Stop this y'all, we got bigger shit going on." Deshawn exhaled and pulled his little brother back by his hood. I laughed at his ass as we headed up the stairs to Cori's apartment.

"Hey y'all," Cori sniffled. I didn't care that she was crying; this bitch was a snake.

"Cori, baby girl, why are all these people saying they working for and with you?" Deshawn asked with a hopeful expression.

I could tell he was silently praying his sister had a good explanation for this shit. Me on the other hand, I felt there was no excuse.

"I don't know Deshawn! I told you that!" she cried, and ran her fingers through her hair. I shook my head because I knew this hoe was lying.

"Cori, please don't lie," Deshawn said.

"I'm not lying! I don't know what the hell is going on! I hate Namiko but not that much!" she yelled, as millions of tears drenched her face. She looked over at me, hoping to get sympathy.

"You a got damn lie!" I yelled punching her wall. "One more thing Cori! One more fucking thing and I'm offing you! I don't care how small it is, and I don't care that your brother is my best friend!" I screamed in her face. "I bet not even find the slightest clue that you had something to do with any of this or I'm taking you out!" I added and quickly left her place. I stormed down the stairs and saw that bitch ass nigga Robbie entertaining some hoe.

"Bye fuck nigga!" he laughed, and so did the girl.

I was gonna walk away but decided against it. I had so much pent up anger that I needed to take out on someone anyway. I stormed back over to him, and he stood up out of his plastic seat. I pulled my gun from my waist, and bitch slapped him to the ground as his little hoe screamed. I cocked my gun and aimed it at his head.

"Talk that shit now nigga," I said through gritted teeth.

"Max!" Deshawn yelled as he ran to me.

He pushed my hand away, and then helped his brother up, whose head was now bleeding. We stared each other down, before Robbie finally walked away at his brother's request. His little hoe was staring me down lustfully, and I just shook my head.

"This ain't over Maximilian!" he yelled, before turning to go up the apartment complex steps. I walked back to the car with Deshawn hot on my heels.

"Yo' family is trying me man," I exhaled and slid down in my seat.

"Just chill my nigga. You on one right now," Deshawn said as he drove to McDonald's to get Evelyn and Aniku's food. They were at the hospital with Namiko still.

"No nigga, you on one if you think Cori ain't have nothing to do with this shit!" I yelled and sat up.

Just then, bullets started flying at our car from every direction possible. We swerved throughout the streets until we finally flew onto a one-way street... going the opposite way.

"Get on the sidewalk!" I yelled just before the car hit a pole, and then collided with an eighteen-wheeler.

# KIYUKI

Namiko was in the hospital, and Max and Deshawn were most likely dead by now; today was a good day as Ice Cube once said. I smiled to myself as I painted my toenails. I get what I want all the time, and when I don't- people have to pay. I tried to warn Max and Namiko, but they just kept ignoring me. I hate to be ignored if you haven't noticed.

As I fanned my polish to dry it up, I heard my doorbell ring. *Odd*, I said to myself. I told Larry I wouldn't be ready to go out until 8pm and it was only 4pm; he was so dumb. I shook my head as I got off the couch.

"Larry, you don't listen boo," I said rolling my eyes as I switched to the door. I smiled and opened it, only to see Cori's big ass.

"What the fuck do you want?" I frowned in disgust. She looked a fucking mess, and her chunky face was covered in tearstains.

"I know you been fucking with me bitch," she said, as she pulled a gun from her jacket and aimed it at me. My eyes got big as shit, as she backed me into the house, and slammed the door behind her.

"Cori wait-"

*POW!*

# Become a VIP Reader!

*To join my mailing list text **SHVONNE** to **66866** and stay up to date! Also, join **Shvonne Latrice Reading Group** on Facebook!*